ALL THE KINGS FALL

ALSO BY A. M. DUNNEWIN

A Cursed Age

All the Dark Souls Trilogy
All the Dark Souls
All the Blood Spilt
All the Kings Fall

The Benighted Saga
The Benighted
The Illusory

Speakeasy Novellas
Speakeasy
Rum Runner

ALL THE KINGS FALL

A NOVEL

A. M. DUNNEWIN

Dark Hour
—PRESS—

First published in the United States of America by A. M. Dunnewin, 2023
Published by Dark Hour Press, LLC, 2023

Published by Dark Hour Press, LLC, California.

www.darkhourpress.com

ISBN: 978-1-952577-19-2

Photograph of sword by Jakub Krechowicz/Shutterstock.com

Cover and jacket design by A. M. Dunnewin

First Edition

For the helpers
who aren't acknowledged,
but are always there regardless.

CHAPTER ONE

"He didn't die. He didn't even flinch."

Joss Brevyn remembered it differently.

As she watched Callan Ronen—lost prince, wanted prisoner—pacing back and forth in front of her, recalling what had happened to them earlier that day in the town of Raspshire, she remembered along with him but with a slightly different perspective. There was the town and its festivities, and then the moment when the hooded figure appeared in the distance and aimed his pistol at Callan. The prince had fled into a tavern; Joss bolted in on horseback and climbed up the stairs where Callan fought his attacker before the masked culprit fled, crashing into a window to escape. She remembered vividly how Callan mounted the saddle behind her, how they cleared the staircase while still on horseback, and when Callan fired at the figure in the doorway. But what she also remembered was how the stranger *had* flinched but didn't fall, remaining on his feet. While a bewildering sight, Joss had been too caught up in trying to escape to dwell on it.

Now, against the darkening twilight with Callan pacing and Henrik Vanzant, her assistant, bent down to start a fire, Joss's mind wandered to the memory of a different conversation.

I'm still going to find you when this is all over.

She clung to those words; she couldn't help herself. Aric Kayden might be an assassin, but to her he was still that injured man on the side of the road, still a mystery despite how clear his intentions had become. Her eyes moved to the bandage around her hand, the green strip of cloth from the cloak he used to wrap around her bruised knuckle. Quietly slipping it off, she found her hand already on the mend and the cloth no longer needed. A bit disappointed, she slipped the cloth into the pocket of her vest, not able to part with it yet.

"Maybe you missed. Maybe you didn't hit him but thought you had," Henrik offered without looking up, striking the flint rock with his dagger to spark a flame.

Joss didn't see how Callan's eyes narrowed, insulted. "I don't miss," he said pointedly.

You swear? She could still hear those words escape her lips, laced in hope, something she hadn't felt in an exceptionally long time.

On my life. The words were so simple yet the impact they left was startling, so much so that she felt them all the way down into her bones. Aric had made a swift exit right afterwards, but he left a heavy impression, one that weighed down on her hours after.

"He must have been wearing some kind of armor, then," Henrik piped up, coming to sit near Joss, which brought her attention back. She brushed a strand of her short, dark brown hair behind her ear, trying to focus on the present rather than the past.

Callan was still pacing. "Obviously," he grumbled, though the way he became lost in thought showed his tone was directed more towards his irritation of not being certain. "He was too fluid to be wearing anything from the armory," he mused, and then he stopped. "Unless…"

Joss and Henrik both looked up, finding him staring out into the dark forest.

"That asshole." It came out as a whisper, and at first Joss didn't know if she heard him right until he spun around, his infamous glare plastered on his face. "He stole it."

"Who? Stole what?" Henrik questioned, an eyebrow arched as he warmed his hands against the glow of the flames.

"Davien. He stole my idea." Callan's shoulders rolled back, his chest puffed out as if the threat had stepped in front of him, his body ready to act. He faced them, blinking, trying to pull himself together. "When I was in training, we wore these thick leather vests to help against attacks. There were a couple of blokes who were… less enthusiastic about following rules."

"So, you had your fair share of bullies once," Henrik smirked, amused. "That would have been entertaining to see."

While a quiet snarl escaped, Callan answered carefully, "They didn't target *me*. They targeted the weaker boys, or at least those they considered weak. One in particular." His voice grew a little softer as he thought back. "They were ruthless to him, unforgiving. He was always being sent to the infirmary. I couldn't personally intervene; the trainers wouldn't allow it. So, I took his leather vest, stole some battered steel blades from the armory that weren't being used, and I broke the blades and sewed them into his vest—"

"You sew?" Henrik gawked, cutting him off. Joss was also a little taken aback by it, her honey-colored eyes staring at the prince, trying to imagine him working a needle and thread.

"After learning how to sew open wounds, anything is fair game," he replied, eyeing them both, knowing that out of anybody, these two would understand. "As I was saying, I tailored his vest, which became a rude awakening to those fools when they tried to combat him in a knife fight. A bullet would have also been blocked."

"Do you think the person back at the tavern was him?" Joss asked out of curiosity.

Schemes can run long and deep sometimes. These were words spoken by Callan himself, back when he was a prisoner standing on trial. It had been poetic at the time but became a harsh truth the longer they knew him.

"It wasn't him," Callan replied, turning away to resume his pacing. "He died in my arms during our first battle at the border wars."

Well, that rules that out, she thought, her gaze falling back to the flames. Her stomach growled, and at first, she thought the nausea was returning until she realized it was hunger. While they had already rationed the food for the evening, it hadn't sufficed. The charcoal Henrik gave her after the poisoning had worn off and now her stomach demanded more food. It didn't help that her side still felt bruised due to the punch from Master Greyson, the executioner who had betrayed them, an injury that had been overshadowed by both the poisoning and the adrenaline rush of trying to survive Raspshire. While no one would have objected if she took more food, Joss decided against it, taking a swig from the canteen instead.

"It could have been anyone at this point," Henrik thought out loud, running a hand through his tousled brown hair, sleep pulling against the sides of his hazel eyes.

"No," Callan replied. "The other man—the one I fought with inside the tavern—wasn't wearing a vest like that. And neither was the man out in the forest who Aric shot."

Joss swallowed the next sip of water hard, wishing Callan hadn't said his name. She wasn't used to being the hopeless romantic; that was her baby sister Celine's forte, not hers. Stepping into her shoes felt awkward and out of place, though secretly she had always wanted a happily ever after, the kind her younger brother Oliver would sometimes write about.

"It had to have been Davien." Callan practically snarled at the thought of his middle brother. "Since he knows I'm the better fighter, he would have copied the vest, that little shit."

The conversation fell into silence, Callan's thoughts keeping him company as he continued pacing, the warrior in him scheming what his next move would be. Henrik, on the other hand, settled down against his saddle, not wanting to fight the sleepiness that was coming for him.

That left Joss, whose gaze flicked periodically between the prince and her assistant. It had been a grueling day for all of them—the fight in Raspshire, the near death of Henrik by one of the masks. She took in a quiet but deep breath as she sat back against her own saddle. Twice, she almost lost Henrik, and while he was safe and sound asleep by her, she couldn't bring herself to put her guard down. Even when a breeze rustled through and the crickets started up, or when the horses stirred in the background, content where they were tied, she couldn't find it in herself to rest.

"I guess I'm not the only one."

Joss looked up into Callan's face as he finally decided to join them, sitting down on the other side of the fire where his saddle waited for him. In the fire light, the dark orbs of his eyes glistened against his umber skin, and he ran his hand through his short, curly black hair, his thoughts still overwhelming him. She didn't have to wonder what he meant, already knowing what really happened to him back in those battles everyone thought had taken him. Sleep would never come easily for either of them.

"How's your shoulder feeling?" she asked, catching him off guard. He'd almost forgotten he had a shoulder injury thanks to one of Aric's arrows. The escape from Galmoor felt far away, given everything that had happened since then.

"Oh... it's fine," Callan replied, rubbing the area to make sure. With a nod, he confirmed everything was still healing well.

Joss grinned, glad to hear it. "Well, at least this is almost over," she reminded them both. "One more night and you'll be home."

A smile was there, but it didn't reach his eyes. While Joss thought for sure he would show some sort of relief, he seemed more hesitant. "Yes," he finally spoke out, as if to finalize it.

Joss eyed him, seeing that while he sounded decided, the way he glanced down at his shirt and pants revealed how self-conscious he was. It didn't help that Master Greyson's blood had dried to a murky brown against his attire, making the clothes look even more dirty and worn.

"They're not going to care what you look like," she offered, causing his eyes to shift to hers. "They'll be too happy to see you alive."

She and Henrik, on the other hand, would be a different story. They hadn't changed their clothes in days, ever since leaving their hometown of Galmoor to track down the prince who sat in front of her. A warm bath and clean clothes were luxuries she craved, looking forward to them once Callan was safely home.

Callan nodded, though he didn't believe her. "I was hoping I'd have a chance to clean myself up at Raspshire; look a little more presentable."

"It matches your story," Joss reminded him. "A man of war missing for almost five years would look a little worse for wear."

Callan's smirk was fleeting. He played with the ends of his sleeves, making sure to keep them down enough to hide the markings on his wrists. "It's just..."

Joss waited, listening to the fire crackle and a light snore escape Henrik.

"My wife," Callan said softly, "I don't know how she's been. I don't know if she's... moved on."

Joss knew that feeling all too well. She tapped a finger against the canteen in thought. "Well, you sent a trinket to her revealing yourself and she sent a pardon. Sounds like if she did move on, she didn't move far."

Callan thought it over. "I guess not," he replied.

Joss watched him for a moment, and seeing him still troubled, decided to pursue one more conversation. "If you don't mind me asking, what was the trinket you sent?"

Callan raised his gaze from the fire, and while the apprehension was still there, he let it go with a deep breath. Grabbing a nearby stick, he came to stand next to Joss, who sat up a little straighter.

In the dirt between her and the fire, he wrote, *Leirum U Oye Voli.*

Joss stared at the words as Callan went back to resume his seat.

"What does it mean?" she asked, causing him to smile in mischief.

"You're smart," he reasoned with a little grin. "You can figure it out."

"You've caught me on an off day." Joss smiled, her exhaustion long set in her eyes.

Callan's smile deepened into a sheepish laugh. "It's 'I love you Muriel' spelled backwards. When we were courting, I wanted to leave her notes without people becoming too suspicious. I'd leave those words on strips of paper, lay them in her favorite books or hide them among the flowers in a garden she visits. Granted, I was sixteen when the idea came to me, thinking I was the cleverest."

Joss laughed a little at the sentiment, though deep down she thought it was cute. She remembered the green cloth in her pocket, a little trinket of her own. "You two courted for a while, then."

"Young love," Callan replied, smiling into the fire. "Everyone thinks we started courting after my training finished and I had a couple battles from the border wars under my belt. But it started when we were younger, secretly hiding those notes. I always knew it would be her."

Joss watched him, feeling a pang of envy creeping in, though she tried to dismiss it as being tired. "That's definitely a trinket worth remembering," she replied quietly.

Callan's smile didn't fade but his enthusiasm did, still worried despite his best efforts to push it off. With nothing more to add, Callan nodded to Joss in good night before lying down.

Joss remained where she was, watching the fire as the night stretched on around them. Crickets fell in tune with the quiet snapping of the flames as the moonlight brushed silver against the treetops. Despite the peace, however, the heaviness persisted in her chest, the remnants of also being afraid that someone she loved would move on without her.

She thought over her last conversation with Aric again, trying to recall his tone, his sincerity, the way he looked at her when he had said it.

On my life.

She kept going back to that moment—over and over again—in hopes history wouldn't repeat itself this time, that he wasn't like all the others. He would come back; he would keep his word.

She kept going back because, deep down, that was all she had left of him.

CHAPTER TWO

The moon hung full overhead as the two riders crashed through the undergrowth, the patchwork of moonlight in between the tree branches showing them the hunter's path they tried to follow. While the main road would have been better for this kind of pace, this particular path was the quickest way over the sharp hills that enclosed the valley where Aselian lay.

They'd started out as three riders, the last who were left from the attacks on Raspshire.

After losing the prince and gaining the attention of the insufferable assassin, the masked figures who remained alive had scattered. It had taken hours, but eventually they regrouped along the edge of the forest, taking inventory of who was left and being left behind. Since there were only three, they could tell themselves apart, brothers from training who knew the voices of their peers. One was hunched over in the saddle, his mask cracked, his side aching, claiming he jumped from a window to escape the prince who had fought as ruthlessly as their leader. The second was out of breath, chased from the town once the assassin picked up on his scent, catching sight of him from a balcony window. A clumsy mistake, he learned, when an arrow scratched the side of his neck as he fled the scene.

Lastly, there was the third rider, sitting up straight and untouchable, the leader who called himself the Mask and was very much annoyed to see that Aric Kayden had decided—again—to not do his job. "Worthless," he grumbled, knowing it would be pointless to persuade the assassin otherwise. No matter, he had decided, flicking his annoyance away as easily as he had flicked his wrist to swat a bug. There were other ways the assassin would be dealt with.

The three had left at a gallop, needing to reach Aselian before dawn. They followed the path, winding through the forested hills that were ascending upward. They should have tracked the prince then; gone back to the main road and hunted them down. But given their positioning and where they had ended up, the three would only waste time, especially since they were down a couple of men. No, they had to get ahead of the prince and those two companions of his to wait for a better opportunity, and then they, too, would be dealt with.

Since their dark masks were still on, none of them were quite sure who exactly was among them. That was the precise reason they wore neutral masks: so they would look unified, undistinguishable. It helped when dealing with an enemy but was a liability when they were amongst themselves.

Especially when a fourth rider had shown up behind them.

Despite the shadows, the quick glimpses over their shoulders revealed he also was wearing a dark mask, his ensemble matching theirs perfectly. The only thing the shadows did conceal was the crossbow slung over his shoulder, hidden by both movement and darkness, as well as his long blond hair concealed under his hood. He matched their pace, keeping the same distance as the others. When time passed and nothing of importance happened, they let him be, their attention pulled more to watching the trail than their own backs.

As they progressed, the fourth rider drew his horse slowly but persistently up next to the man whose neck still bore the arrow's scratch. There was no hesitation when the fourth rider threw his fist towards him, a knife clasped in his grip. The blade sunk into the man's neck, right where the arrow should have gone, hitting his mark hours later. A gurgled cry escaped before the knife was yanked out, blood squirting into the air. The body bobbed along with the horse's rhythm until finally being thrown from the saddle, the horse slowing its pace as if realizing it was free of its rider.

The murderous sounds, however, didn't escape the next rider, whose cracked mask turned to catch a glimpse of the commotion. Seeing the riderless horse, he panicked, kicking his steed in hopes to outrun the threat. Unfortunately, that's what the attacker had predicted. With his horse's momentum already in his favor, he pressed on, gaining on the rider who was now calling out to his superior.

"Sir!" he yelled, his voice loud but muffled behind the mask as he tried to gain attention, tried to get help. He glanced over, finding to his dismay that his opponent had caught up to him. He swung his arm out, trying to fight him off, which only made him cry out as his bruised side raged in pain from the movement.

"Sir, *please!*" he screamed, and in his voice wasn't the call from a comrade but the shrill cry for help from a scared young man.

The leader in front only looked back once, and in response, he dug his heels into his steed and pressed on.

The two horses remained side by side, and as the scared masked man swung his arm again, his opponent grabbed his wrist. In a blink, the knife blade slid deep into the armpit. Although the masked man cried out, he was already growing faint from blood loss when he was pulled off the saddle. Hitting the ground, he tumbled against the dirt floor while his horse slowed, realizing he, too, was free.

Picking up the reins he dropped, Aric Kayden set his sights on the last rider. Needing to see better, he tore off the mask he wore, losing it as it slipped from his grasp while pushing his horse forward. He knew his own horse was tired—it had already been a hell of a day and an even longer night—but given how the last man had called out to his superior, Aric assumed the remaining rider was none other than the Mask.

The Mask who had paid him to hunt down a man who ended up being the lost prince.

The Mask who had tortured him when he refused to kill his mark.

The Mask who would go after Jocelyn and Henrik next, if he didn't get his way.

Fuck you and your name, Aric growled at him as he brought his crossbow around, an arrow already locked in the chamber.

The trail twisted, trees closing in on them, making it hard to take a good shot. Aric was familiar with this area though, remembering how the trees would clear and they'd reach the top of the hill that would look down on Aselian. He would have his chance, and everything would be over. The Mask would be dead, the prince would make it home safely, and then there would be Jocelyn, safe and sound and *his*. He didn't even care if they went back to the wretched countryside after all this; he just wanted her.

As predicted, the trees fanned out and the clearing came, the peak of the hill now before them in a dark, silver heap. Taking aim, Aric pulled the trigger, and the arrow found its mark perfectly in the rider's back. He automatically smirked in satisfaction until he realized the Mask, despite the typical flinch of being hit, hadn't fallen from his horse.

A curse did escape, also typical, but otherwise he seemed unfazed. *Too* unfazed, as if the arrow hadn't actually hit him.

What the hell? Aric seethed, shouldering his crossbow and pushing his horse more urgently forward.

As much as his horse tried, the Mask had a more rested steed, allowing the distance to grow between them. Aric cursed, trying to urge his horse over the hill, but once they made it, the Mask and his horse were lost in the darkness.

Pulling on the reins, he let his horse rest as he scoured the area, listening, searching. Phantom sounds of hooves pounded against the earth, but they vanished before he could find the direction they had gone.

Shit. Aric huffed out, the exhaustion finally settling in. He pulled his gaze from the dark forest and settled it on the kingdom of Aselian, nestled against the lake, the beginning of the river that followed the main road in and out of the valley. From where he sat, he saw the lights shimmering against the water, glowing like a beacon of hope. He still felt a swell of excitement of being home, back in the city that breathed without pause, day or night. There was never a dull moment, never a job that didn't need to be done. The court life with its intrigue and alluring possibilities had always been his playground, his love life.

As he sat there, his grey and green eyes staring down at the areas of the kingdom he knew best, Aric couldn't help but look in the direction of the main road, knowing who was traveling on it; who he had made a promise to. Absent-mindedly, his hand traced the part of his shoulder where the stitches were still in place, as if feeling Jocelyn's touch binding him back together.

I've beheaded someone I loved before, and I can't do it again.

Those words had been driving him mad ever since she said them in the tavern in Greywall. Her honesty caused him to want her more, to prove to her that she didn't need to fear the future when it came to him. He'd find her when this was all over, no matter how much they were driven apart, and he'd spend the rest of his life showing her how much she wouldn't regret loving him. He'd promised, and he intended to keep that promise.

But while his feelings were strong for her, a small part of him questioned if he really could give up his old life for a new one.

CHAPTER THREE

"But he *could* wake up."

The two physicians exchanged glances, and Muriel knew that between their stares all hope was lost.

"He's comfortable," one of them confirmed, turning to smile reassuringly at the queen. "All we can do is wait and see."

Charisse—the second wife of King Lyson Ronen—smiled back as if she had stated a fact. If she thought and prayed hard enough, her husband lying in front of her would prove her right. For a split second, Muriel saw where Davien inherited his grandiose thinking from.

As the physicians saw themselves out, Muriel remained standing to the side, watching as the king lay sunken in his bed. The bed sheets were still folded neatly in place, covering him up to his chest with his hands lying listless on either side of him.

Charisse's jeweled hands found his as she sat back down in the chair next to his bedside. The bright fuchsia and violet of her jeweled gown counteracted the solemness of the room, and Muriel had to look away, her eyes drawing to the window as if getting a breath of fresh air.

She could see the ripples in the lake the castle backed up to, the hills and mountain peaks jetting up into the sky in the distance. Another morning had gone by in silence of Callan's whereabouts, or news from Callan himself. After last night and witnessing Davien's takeover into becoming regent, Muriel felt like she had been scraped empty on the inside. Even her appearance showed it: her dark mauve gown was plain compared to the queen's ensemble, and her lack of jewelry simplified her look. Her thick, curly black hair was braided back. She hadn't wanted to bother with it.

As she stared out at those mountains, the doors opened, and she heard Davien's voice as his footsteps echoed into the room.

"Any signs yet?" he questioned as the doors closed behind him. No greeting; just facts.

Muriel shuddered as if the words were crawling against the back of her neck. She still couldn't forgive what she had seen the previous night in the meeting hall, lying on the ground in between the benched rows and listening to the council install Davien as regent. It was a simple political tactic, a way to get a stronger standing as being made king in case anyone questioned him. Or, worse for him, if Callan returned.

Thinking of her husband made her eyes mist over, and so like all the times before, she swatted his memory away so she could think clearly. She had to; it hadn't done her any good those first couple of years he was missing, and now all anyone ever saw in her was a running joke. The sad princess; the wife without a husband. And that's only if they weren't trying to find some scandal involving her to amuse themselves.

"He's comfortable," Charisse spoke up, reiterating the doctor's words. "I'm sure he's just over exhausted and needs his rest. The news of Callan must have overexcited him."

"News. What news?" Davien replied, and the coldness in his tone caught Muriel's attention, prompting her to swing her gaze at him.

"That Callan might have been found," his mother replied, looking at him as if it were absurd that he could have forgotten.

"Ah, well," Davien replied, his pointed look falling on Muriel. "We know who's responsible for all this, then."

Muriel's jaw dropped open, seeing the threat. Yes, she had been the one to send out the criers and pardon without authorization, but the king had understood her motives. However, the idle gossip throughout the years hadn't helped her relationship with the queen. Charisse never took kindly to anything that might tarnish the reputation of *her* family, and since Callan was her stepson and half-brother to her boys, Muriel was nothing more than a liability. King Lyson had always stood up for her, knowing Muriel since she was a child, but things had changed, years gone by, and now the only person who could vouch for her was silent.

"Enough," Charisse hissed, surprising both of them. She had taken the king's hand, was pressing it to her cheek. "He just wants one of his sons back."

"You're siding with her?" Davien gawked, still not over the conversation.

"You're not a parent. You don't understand." Charisse kept her eyes on her husband, and Muriel felt a pang of sympathy, understanding the pain and frustration of being unable to reach the man she loved. "Besides, Lyson was right," she continued, "I would have done the same thing, sending those criers out."

Davien was about to object again, but the doors behind him opened, hushing his remarks.

Another set of footsteps entered, followed by a cheerful tone none of them expected to hear.

"The prodigal son has returned," the man boosted, coming to stand next to Davien. Patting him on the back in teasing, he turned towards the rest of them, his tone sobering a little at the sight of his father. "Any changes yet?" he asked a little more sympathetically.

"Eiden," Charisse smiled at her youngest as she rested her husband's hand back on the bed. "When did you arrive?"

"Not that long ago," he reassured her, and although he smiled back, the way his eyes diverted back to his father gave away that he was still looking for an answer.

"He's going to be fine," Charisse reassured him, but when she looked away, Eiden's eyes found Muriel, who shook her head softly.

Eiden nodded once, still catching the attention of Davien who just missed their exchange.

Muriel tried to hide her smile. Eiden matched his brother in looks—short curly sable hair, light brown skin—but his personality was the complete opposite. It seemed where Davien's personality ended, Eiden's began, a much lighter version than his brother.

"You didn't have to travel all the way over here," Charisse continued. "I know training comes first in all things."

"Training is an undertaking, but nothing I can't handle." He smiled suavely as he walked around to the other side of the bed.

"Second time's a charm," Davien pointed out smugly.

"You'd know since you're always second best," Eiden jabbed back. "You never were able to beat Callan's records. Excellent job, brother," he mocked.

"And you have?" Davien raised an eyebrow, curious but cautious. The jealousy was beginning to show.

"I don't bother with records," Eiden admitted off-handedly. "They don't often protect you in battle."

It was the one smart thing he had said, but then again, Eiden usually said things that were smart but often dismissed. His flippant attitude and toxicity with women alone gave him a rogue status he hadn't been able to shake, not that he bothered to try. It amused him that people thought so lowly of him, possibly because everyone thought so highly of his brothers. Well, one of them, and he had been missing for years.

"They help in other aspects," Davien countered, standing up a little too proudly.

"I'm sure they do, *regent*," Eiden winked, mocking his brother and the news he had already been told.

Davien was about to counteract the slight when their mother hushed them. "Boys, enough," Charisse groaned, keeping her gaze on her husband. "If you're going to bicker, do it elsewhere. Your father doesn't need to hear it."

Muriel watched as the two exchanged harsh glances. As if bored with the idea that he wouldn't be able to harass his brother anymore, Eiden moved away from the bed. "Apologies, mother. I better be going anyway. I have some princely duties to attend to."

"Oh yes, I'm sure those harlots need attending," Davien mumbled.

Eiden smirked as he rounded past his brother and made his way to Muriel. "Sister." He smiled in both greeting and farewell, kissing her cheek before winking at her. Turning away, he replied lightly, "And don't forget the wine, brother. Need to get my fill in before you abolish it like you will anything fun."

Eiden left the room with a chuckle, and Muriel pressed her lips together so she wouldn't laugh along with him.

In Eiden's place came one of Davien's companions, a knight who had stood by his side in the meeting hall, causing Muriel's hidden smile to fade. The knight had no business being there, and by how he acted, he didn't want to be either. He immediately went to Davien, whispered something in his ear, and then hurried back out.

The change was drastic, the harsh lines in Davien's face becoming harder.

"Excuse me, mother. I have some things to attend to as well." He bowed before Charisse could acknowledge him, and only a glare at Muriel sufficed as a farewell.

Muriel watched him go, curious as to why he was acting more concerned while leaving than when he arrived.

Knowing it would be better to leave Charisse alone than stay with her, Muriel quietly made her way to the door. But before leaving entirely, she turned back to face the king's bed where he remained unconscious next to his wife.

"Thank you for earlier, Your Majesty," Muriel said softly as she bowed, alluding back to Davien's earlier accusation.

"It wasn't for you." Charisse turned a hard look towards her, and that was the expression Muriel knew so well. "The duty of a queen is to always make sure the king's image is untarnished—is favored—no matter the gossip."

Muriel swallowed hard, knowing another rumor must have been circling. That, or Davien had said something to his mother about making Muriel his wife, a long-running threat which was becoming more real by the day. "I understand," she reassured her, though Callan was the only king she had in mind.

"I'm glad you do." Charisse nodded, though her expression didn't change. "Because no matter your feelings, you must always stand beside him. You must always uphold his image. It takes an extraordinarily strong man to hold the burdens of being king. It takes an equally strong woman to share in carrying that weight."

He had told her. Muriel felt it in her chest by how her heart pounded away, the corner of her eye twitching though she tried to blink away so it wouldn't show. Davien was no longer just threatening her; he had gained an ally in his mother. No matter how begrudging she was towards it, it was only a matter of time until Muriel would be forced to decide and suffer the consequences. She already knew she'd say no; she just didn't know how vengeful his spite would be afterwards. So far it had been a dangerous dance between them, a cat-and-mouse game where Davien planned to force her to take his hand. She was a little scared to know what he'd do with her once it occurred to him that he couldn't win this game, that he could never have her.

Muriel slipped out of the room, making her way back to her chambers. Her ladies-in-waiting would have greeted her out in the hall, but she had dismissed them earlier that morning, not wanting to bore them with her routine. They were always around first thing in the morning and in the evenings to help her get ready for supper and then bed, and sometimes they would go with her to the cathedral to pray. But Muriel had made her routine so basic that she decided not to drag them into it, allowing them to have lives when she couldn't. It also didn't help overhearing one of the girls gloating about being with one of Davien's men. That made distancing herself a little easier.

Walking the corridor alone, she passed by sconces burning with electrical light, showing her the way. A couple of guards passed her in the hall, bowing to her before continuing on to relieve those at the king's door.

Muriel was approaching another hallway when she overheard someone speak out, their words lost by distance. Coming to a halt, she heard another sharp whisper, a demand.

Inching closer, she came to where the halls met, pressing herself against the wall. Carefully, she looked around the corner, finding Davien and his friend a little ways down. Davien's fists were locked on the man's collar, his friend staring at him in a mixture of shock and shame.

"What do you mean he's here?" Davien seethed, his face close to the knight's.

"H—He was spotted near the outpost," the man stammered. "He might be entering Aselian anytime. We had no warning—"

"There were plenty of warnings!" Davien yelled, pushing his friend away. His hands immediately went to his forehead as he started pacing, something Muriel had never seen him do before.

"We didn't know it was really him," the knight tried to defend. "So many people have come forward pretending to be Callan Ronen—"

"*She* sent a pardon!" Davien snapped, his eyes squeezing shut, his rage manifesting in his ever-tightening fist that shook as he paced the floor. "She sent criers, so she knows it's him—" he growled the rest of the words "—which means he's *alive!*"

Callan! Her mind screamed, and she had to clamp her hands over her mouth as she moved back, leaning against the wall to steady herself.

"He's not alone."

Muriel heard Davien stop short, and when she peeked again, her mouth still covered and her heart pounding in her ears, she saw him slowly look at his knight.

"Two others are with him," the knight spoke up, standing his ground against the prince's icy glare.

"So, he made friends," Davien thought out loud, rubbing his jaw in thought. "Keep everyone on alert. The minute he's spotted again, find me. I want to deal with him myself."

Davien marched off in the opposite direction, the knight following a couple paces behind.

Muriel stared at the two men as they vanished around a corner, eyes wide as she lowered her hand, her body trembling. *He's alive.* Her mind looped back, a smile forming through her gasps, tears springing to her eyes.

He was alive, and she had been right. Muriel looked both ways then, realizing she was by herself, still alone with this knowledge.

When she bolted into a run, needing to get to her chambers

quickly, it was out of a different type of desperation. Callan was alive and she needed to find him first, to get to him before Davien.

25

CHAPTER FOUR

As was their routine, Joss and the others woke early, saddling the horses and making their way back onto the hunter's path. They had found it while fleeing on the main road, using it to find refuge in the forest for the night. Retracing their steps, they came upon the road and followed it in the direction of Aselian.

As the path curved into the forest, the hills became more pronounced as they rose tall overhead. The trees eventually fanned out, and the three soon found themselves facing a vast river with sharp-edged cliffs rising against the shores, cradling the water that moved in a serpentine fashion. The road squeezed itself between water and earth, and the trio followed along the winding path at a steady pace. Ships sailed past, some leaving while another was heading in the same direction they were going.

"Too bad we can't get a ride with them," Henrik commented, watching as the ship easily passed them by.

"Too bad," Callan murmured, and Joss sensed he was still apprehensive. She couldn't blame him; he'd been gone almost five years without any word from his family. After everything he had been through, nothing would ever be quite the same again.

There wasn't much small talk as they pushed the horses back into a gallop, passing other travelers who were friendly enough but still hadn't recognized Callan. Leery of it, Joss wondered if anyone would ever recognize him or if that would be another battle they'd have to contend with, proving who he was.

Shaking her head at the thought, she focused on the path before them, trying not to get ahead of herself. She knew she was exhausted, her side and stomach still sore, and it didn't help that the nervousness of reaching Aselian was weighing on her. It couldn't be forgotten that this was the same royal line who forced the Brevyns into being executioners, the downfall of her family. Joss didn't like how that sat in her stomach each time she thought of Callan being king—how desperation twisted itself into her gut in wanting to know if he'd pardon her and Henrik. It was something everyone in her family had begged for. Even Master Greyson had believed it as a solid outcome before being killed.

Not quite the pardon he was looking for, she thought to herself as she followed her companions around another sharp bend. While the scene remained fuzzy to her, thanks to the poison Master Greyson forced her to drink, she could still see the blood spattered on the rocky shore of the river, causing her stomach to turn in remembrance of it.

"I'm going to need some new clothes," Callan decided, breaking into Joss's thoughts.

"Don't we all," Henrik pointed out, causing the prince to look back at him. The lad lifted an arm to display his own worn-through attire.

"You look fine. *I'm* the one people will be looking at." Callan turned back around and trudged forward, pushing his horse into a trot.

"I kind of hate that he's right," Henrik mumbled as Joss rode up next to him, the two keeping pace as they, too, trotted forward to stay up with the prince.

"I'm sure we have enough coins to at least get clean shirts," Joss pointed out. They'd eventually have to anyway; cleaning their shirts would be pointless, given how stained they were.

"Better than nothing," Henrik smirked at her, but after a moment it disappeared under a furrowed look.

"What's wrong?" she asked, wondering if he was thinking back on Elora Tansy again, her act of betrayal hitting him deeply.

"What if he doesn't pardon us," Henrik whispered above the noise of the clopping hooves.

So, she wasn't the only one contemplating it.

"We didn't expect him to," Joss reminded him, keeping her voice down as well. Callan was a distance away, and despite his exceptional hearing, they hoped the noises from the horses would drown out their words.

"Yeah, but..." Henrik trailed off.

"I know," Joss agreed, ending the conversation as they watched Callan pull his horse back down to a walk while waiting for them.

Reaching him, they found him pointing off to the distance where the main road fanned out, the cliffs subsiding into a cove where the forest took over. On the edges of the trees was a modest cluster of buildings, a small outpost just before the main road curved behind another cliff, which rose to resume its barrier against the river's edge.

"There's one this close to Aselian?" Henrik asked.

"Lookouts," Callan replied. "Given how winding the road is, it was originally put here to help warn Aselian of any oncoming attacks. Now it's used as a base for caravans and travelers to regroup. We might be able to find a vendor here."

Without waiting for the others to agree, Callan made the decision for them by pushing his horse forward, forcing the other two to follow. They rode in silence, deciding to keep the ride at a brisk walk to avoid unwanted attention.

During this lull, Callan sat rigidly in his seat, which told Joss something was on his mind. She didn't press him; only followed along with him and Henrik, allowing Callan time to confront his own thoughts. She assumed it had to do with being so close to home and all the what ifs he'd be faced with.

"If I may ask a favor of both of you," he finally spoke up, drawing their attention. "I'd appreciate it if you didn't tell anyone what I told you, about what really happened to me. The story I told those men back in Galmoor is what I need people to believe."

Joss observed his mind ticking away, remembering he had been on trial for murder once, an entire council—although small—being told an altered version of what really happened. In Galmoor, he made it sound like he was in control, fighting in the border wars while his reports weren't being sent back, leading to a greater scheme amongst his men that left one of his own dead and him in jail. But the truth had been much darker and less controlled, a story a future king would be embarrassed to tell. Being captured during a battle was humiliating; being tortured and witnessing what he had seen in those short years bordered on not only horrific but shameful. Kings weren't supposed to be prisoners of war. A certain amount of sympathy would be given to him, but then the questions would begin: who would trust his judgments, especially during times of war? Was Callan Ronen even fit to rule?

Joss saw those questions in his eyes before he batted them away, his typical hard gaze returning as he looked to both for a response.

"We won't tell," Joss assured him, Henrik shaking his head next to her to emphasize his stance.

Callan breathed out hard, much like he had before those four councilmen—releasing the tension bubbling up inside him. "Thank you," he replied softly, sincerely.

The three fell silent again as the buildings loomed ahead, coming upon the sight of a bustling outpost. Wagons were stationed outside of the town, a wagon train preparing to leave. As they rode past, they caught the attention of a few passersby but were soon forgotten as they continued, coming to a hitching post that had become vacant.

Dismounting, they tied the horses and were just untying the saddle bags for safekeeping when someone called out in the distance, their tone sharp against the backdrop of travelers who were frequenting the shops and taverns. The call wasn't to them, but both Henrik and Joss stopped, listening while Callan obliviously staked out the nearest shop.

"Might try one over there first," Callan commented, not realizing Henrik and Joss were in the middle of untying, both staring at each other as if to verify they had heard the voice right.

Then, it came again.

"Nellie the queen, you must keep up!" the voice beckoned in a sing-song fashion, followed by laughter of different voices.

Celine the queen, are you finished yet...

The memory of her younger brother teasing their sister snapped her awake. Joss moved her gaze behind Henrik, searching for him like she did in the taverns. That same emotion overtook her when she would search the Lost Wall, waiting to find a parchment with his likeness etched in ink. When her gaze fluttered back to Henrik, she saw his mirrored expression, confirming they both knew who it was—a voice neither of them had heard in years, a mannerism they hadn't known was lost until it was found.

She didn't know why she rounded past Drakon, was unsure why she felt the need to see him with her own eyes. But when that call came again and the owner came into view, she stopped suddenly, the world stopping with her.

"Joss," Henrik whispered, trying to get her attention back, but it was too late. She had seen him, and only one name screamed in her mind when she recognized those same features, seeing the resemblance of both her mother and father in them.

Oliver.

CHAPTER FIVE

Aselian was bustling as usual, and Aric rode down the main strip of road with a sense of ease like someone who had arrived home. The swindling and bickering, the mixtures of cooking meats and veggies from the vendors—it all played into the nostalgia he missed. The crowds were where he felt at peace, the noises and strayed attentions allowing him to pass without pause. Large groups made things more intimate; conversations were drowned out, faces easily overlooked. The more people, the better. This had allowed him to do his job plenty of times without witnesses. A simple slip of the knife in the right spot would have his victims bleeding out before anyone realized a murder had taken place. By then, he was always long gone.

But no matter how good it was to be back on these streets, re-familiarizing himself with his old haunts, Aric found he was looking for *her*. Any dark hair he saw, especially short, made him take a second glance, showing it wasn't Jocelyn—either by looks or who they were frequenting with. Henrik would have been right by her side, and no doubt that prince too, the three needing to stay together to finish what they had started. There were no signs of either man, and every breath-catching moment he had when he thought he saw her only revealed he hadn't.

Shaking his head, Aric rode past the familiar buildings, meandering around pedestrians, riders, and those who decided to make the street their gathering. He had gone back during the night and found one of the masked men's horses, which he sold to a traveling wagon that needed an extra horse. With the coins firmly in his pocket, Aric moved carefully through the street, taking his time, making sure no attention came to him. Just another man on another horse.

Finding the street he wanted, he rode to a familiar stable, stashing the horse, crossbow, and quiver, and hushed the caretaker up with a couple extra coins.

"Thank you, sir. No one will disturb that stall," the man reassured him before scurrying away.

While he would have preferred to keep his favorite weapon on him, Aric didn't want to run the risk of being easily found, especially if he was being followed. Checking to make sure Jocelyn's kitchen knife was still snug in his boot, he proceeded back onto the street, journeying left until he reached another street and found the building he wanted.

The brothel looked no different than when he had last left it. Some of the girls were on the balcony, skimpily clad despite the chill in the air for being noon, foretelling the seasons were in the midst of changing.

Aric already knew where the training grounds were, the place where the princes and those masked goons learned their tactics. Everyone knew where it was, nestled up in the hills to the north. It was a treacherous road to get there—exactly the reason it was chosen for a training school—and he assumed it wasn't worth the hassle. Obviously, the masked hooligans were in the city, given their presence in the last twenty-four hours, and there was no point making the journey since it would take a couple of days to reach the place anyway.

The one piece of information he did use to his benefit was the brothel. While Callan was dead set on Davien Ronen being his enemy—which wasn't a far-off theory; nobody liked the brute—Aric had been quietly contemplating the next in line to the throne: Eiden Ronen. He remembered that the prince liked brothels, which was a nice but unnecessary tidbit he learned back at the campfire, when Callan was divulging the rules of Mors Exitus. Aric had his own fair share of romps in brothels, and the girls were never quiet when the youngest prince was around, which had been annoying but hey, gossip sometimes came with the price. Often, after some tough jobs, Aric was happy for the distraction. Sometimes, he even used it to his own advantage.

The gossip usually held nothing of real importance, but as Aric made his way across the street, he did his best to think back over it, combing through any details that should have stood out. Eiden was a young, vivacious, and often demanding lover, a hats-off to the fact he was related to an absolute prick of a brother. *And half-brother*, he thought back, Callan's arrogance coming to mind. He still couldn't unsee him at the river, dripping with blood as the rock remained tight in hand after he killed the executioner. Well deserving, given what the bloke had done to Jocelyn, but still. His rage was a little unsettling, and Aric was glad he had given the revolver to Henrik.

Crossing the threshold, he didn't bother removing his hood as he entered the dimly lit dwelling. His eyes adjusted to meet the sitting room where customers were entertained for free, flirting with harlots while listening to some musicians strumming away in a corner and drinking cheap liquor. The good stuff was always reserved for the back room where the higher ends of the kingdom would meet, separated by wealth and walls.

Sweeping past the plush decor, the chandelier buzzing with electrical light overhead, he could smell the booze in the air, the sweat from the working class, and the faint aroma of cigar smoke edging its way in from the back room. Aric always thought it ironic that they separated the customers by class. It shouldn't have mattered; they all ended upstairs anyway.

Approaching the bar, Aric ordered a whiskey from the bartender, who was a fresh face in the area. Aric remained polite, paying for his drink, and taking a hearty swig. But as the bartender moved away to attend to more guests, Aric eyed him, wondering what had happened to the last guy. They hadn't known each other personally, but that bartender had been personable, nodding to him like he did with all the regulars.

Before spiraling further into what-ifs and conspiracies, someone tapped Aric on the shoulder. Begrudgingly, he turned to find the face of someone who did look familiar.

"And where exactly have you been?"

Aric smiled down at the harlot, her features breathtaking in the way she wore her hair and makeup, how the soft lighting touched her features—or by how the whiskey was already affecting him on an empty stomach, he couldn't rule that one out.

"Andrina," he smiled, finding that months apart hadn't changed her or the look she gave him whenever he'd visit.

He watched her gaze flicker back and forth, from his grey eye to the green one. "I missed you," she whispered only for him to hear.

The words didn't quite hit him the way they used to. Granted, he had never been in love with her, but there was an attraction they had both fed on over the last couple of years. Despite their history, however, something had changed. It wasn't until Aric thought he saw a woman come in with short dark hair, his chest thumping in anticipation as he did a double take, that he realized what that change was.

"Everything all right?" Andrina asked, moving a soft blonde curl away from her face, the thin strap of her dress draping off her shoulder from her movements that she didn't bother to fix. The fabric was thin, only held in place by the tightly laced corset which accented her body perfectly.

"Always," Aric recovered, turning on a smile and making sure his eyes didn't divert again.

"Let's go upstairs then," Andrina smiled, taking his hand and leading him to the far staircase like she'd always done.

Aric sucked in a deep breath to calm his nerves, and as he moved along with her up the stairs, he couldn't stop from looking back, making sure for good measure that the person he saw wasn't Jocelyn. Because he already admitted to himself that if it had been her, he would have let go of Andrina's hand in an instant, without a second thought.

CHAPTER SIX

Muriel shut the door to her chambers, glad to be alone. By how she dismissed them, thinking she'd be in the king's chambers longer, she wasn't expecting her ladies-in-waiting to show up for another couple of hours, and that was only if they wanted to attend the cathedral with her. Pressing her back against the door, they were already out of her mind as Muriel relived the conversation she overheard.

He's alive.

She hadn't dreamt it; it had been real. Callan was almost home, and he wasn't by himself. And if he was alive and had traveled this far, then that meant the strangers were helping him.

He's alive, he's going to make it in time!

If only the king could hold on just a little longer.

Muriel began to pace, knowing she needed to help but having no idea how. Her hands twisted together as she walked, feeling both rejuvenated and helpless.

I need to find him first, she thought, the idea causing her to feel more empowered. She had a purpose now, and Callan was almost home.

Running to the pillowcase, she dug out the cloth with those blood-written words on it. *Leirum U Oye Voli.* He hadn't forgotten her.

She was stuffing it into the front of her bodice, keeping it close to her heart, when the idea occurred.

The wall. I can walk the battlements.

She almost gasped in excitement, her emotions tumbling away with her. She hadn't felt this good in a long time, livened by the possibilities that this nightmare would soon be over.

"I'll walk the battlements. No one will think it strange," she was mumbling to herself as she went to her armoire and dug around for a cloak. "I'm just taking a walk. It's as innocent as that."

She smiled as she pulled a deep violet cloak out and wrapped it around her shoulders. Tying the front, she imagined it all so perfectly: she'd walk the battlements that outlined the castle, keep herself at a stroll so the patrolling guards would think she was out for fresh air. She had walked the high walls hundreds of times before. This would look no different, except this time Callan would see her. He'd storm the gates, the guards would recognize their prince, and then she'd see him, and run into his arms. The look on Davien's face would be priceless and then the bells would be rung, proclaiming Callan's return—

Suddenly, Muriel saw the plot hole, causing her arms to drop to her side, a pensive look staining her face. She had to have an escort. She never walked the wall without someone, and normally the escort was her ladies-in-waiting.

Damn it. Now she wished she hadn't dismissed them.

"They better be in the library," she grumbled to herself, knowing a handful of places the girls would be, keeping themselves preoccupied. Tidying herself up in the mirror, she trotted to the door before checking herself over again. She had been upset and downcast for so long that any smiles or happiness would look suspicious, sending the rumor mills spinning. She couldn't allow that kind of attention to fall on her, not with Davien's desperation in play.

Taking in a deep breath, she mentally checked herself, put on her best solemn look, and opened the door.

What was met on the other side caused the gasp to escape involuntarily, and she had to cover her mouth so she wouldn't full-on scream.

"Scare you?" Davien questioned, his eyes looking her over as he stood there, hands clasped in front of him.

Oh God, does he know I heard him?

Muriel stood up a little straighter, trying to compose herself. "It's a normal reaction when someone is caught lurking in doorways."

Davien grinned, though it didn't soften his eyes. "Where are you headed?"

Muriel was about to divulge her whereabouts when something stopped her. What if he followed and saw Callan first? What if her reunion with her husband was nothing more than a trap?

"I'm headed to the cathedral," she lied, not wanting to take any chances.

"This early?" he questioned suspiciously, knowing full well her routine: mornings were for the king, afternoons were for prayers.

Muriel gritted her teeth but tried to act polite. "The king needs more prayers today."

Davien watched her, and it took a while for her story to be believed as he moved to the side to let her pass. "Well, in that case," he added as she stepped out into the hall and turned to close her door, "I'll join you."

Muriel's pulse quickened as her hand tightened on the door handle before letting go. "Wonderful," she smiled, knowing if she balked, then he'd only become more suspicious. "A son should pray for his father."

Davien ignored her, lifting his arm up. "Shall we?" he offered.

Muriel looked at his arm and then back to him. With a smile, she denied it by walking forward, keeping her eyes level on the hallway ahead as he came to match her pace right next to her.

Whether Callan was almost home or not, she wasn't going to be caught dead with her arm linked with a man who could very much ruin her—and her husband's—life. She hoped Callan wouldn't see them together, though; that he'd make his way straight to the castle and take his rightful place.

And, above all else, she hoped Davien wouldn't know until it was too late.

CHAPTER SEVEN

Oliver hadn't changed; not enough to look unrecognizable, at least.

He was still a good foot shorter than their older brother, Flynn, his stature athletic but not muscular, not like the executioners in their family. He abandoned them before that could happen.

His hair was still the same shade as hers, though a bit longer than before. While the Oliver she grew up with had been broody with a head full of stories, the Oliver in front of her was more playful and lighthearted. For a moment Joss thought she was seeing the real side of him, the one where he wasn't the son of an executioner and lived a normal life. In that fleeting moment, she was glad he had left, thankful she found him in this state.

And then the little girl came running up into his arms, a proud smile forming on his face that only a father could have, and suddenly Joss's world cracked. He had left his old family to make a new one. While she had always been an outsider, it was the first time she actually felt like one, peering at the type of life she wanted but couldn't have.

Joss hated that feeling, and she moved forward to take back the distance between them.

Henrik's attention followed her as Callan looked over and realized something was happening. "Where are you going?" he asked.

Joss didn't hear the question as she pulled her hood on, drawing closer without being noticed. The last time she saw Oliver, they had talked about the garden, about how they were going to get the ground ready. The next morning, he disappeared; no note, no goodbye. She had made herself sick with worry over him, had even gone in search of him, until she learned that he had been planning his departure for some time.

He had been gone so long that he didn't even know about Celine yet.

Something tugged on her arm, pulling her back to the present as she heard Henrik whisper, "Don't do this. He's not worth chasing."

"I just want to talk," she replied simply, gently yet confidently pulling her arm free from him.

As she trudged forward, she could hear Callan and Henrik behind her, though she didn't pay attention to them. Oliver sat the little girl down, and that's when she saw how much his daughter resembled him and the rest of the family. Her heart ached, seeing a resemblance to Celine who had the same enthusiasm. She remembered Oliver at that age too, how Flynn and she would have to take turns keeping tabs on him since he was prone to finding hiding spots to write his moody poems and endless stories. That should have been a sign of what was to come, she had realized much later on.

Joss watched as the little girl ran off to join the group they were traveling with, and Oliver called out that he would be right back. He jogged off in the opposite direction, passing the buildings and journeying into the forest. Knowing no one was paying any attention to her, Joss followed.

There were only a couple reasons why he'd go wandering back into the forest: he'd either forgotten something or was off to relieve himself like most did before a long journey. Joss wasn't thrilled about the possibility of the latter, but at least there would be more privacy.

Keeping her distance from him, she strolled in the same direction, her eyes trained on him as she ventured off to the side so it wasn't so obvious she was following. He looked back only once, but his gaze went in the direction of his daughter. The thought still made Joss feel uneasy, the tightness in her chest mimicking how the poison had felt when it started taking effect.

By the time Joss noticed they were far enough from the buildings to not be seen, she lost sight of him. All around were nothing but tall pines and the chirping of birds, an occasional rattle of branches as a squirrel leapt from branch to branch. Looking in the direction she last saw him, she decided it was now or never. Traveling forward, she made her way over, finding only trees and ferns covering any attempt at finding a trail.

Joss was scouting the area for any signs of breakage in the overgrowth when something broke behind her, a twig snapping under the weight of a boot, followed by the cocking of a pistol. She froze, swallowing hard at her mistake.

"Thought you could come out here and rob me, huh?"

That was his voice, the familiar anger coming back into his tone. Joss cringed a little at both the memory and the accusations. He hadn't *seen* her. She was just another person in the crowd.

"Got nothing to say for your actions?" he demanded, taking a step closer.

"I could ask you the same thing," she replied, slowly taking off her hood as she rotated, meeting the sight of the end of the pistol before staring right at Oliver.

The realization came to him slowly, evident by how his eyes widened and his face fell. The pistol slipped down, and by how he was gawking, it wasn't by choice, only surprise.

"Jocelyn," he whispered.

Hearing him say her name felt different than when Aric said it. It was like something horrifying, a ghost from his past.

His eyes haven't changed, her mind pinpointed as she stared into his gaze, which was the same shade of honey brown as hers.

"You know, if you didn't want to help me with the garden, you could have just told me," she tried to tease, lifting a smile to ward off the tension.

He blinked at her, confused.

God, he doesn't even remember. Joss's throat tightened with emotion, and she forced herself to take a deep breath, to stay calm.

"You're not supposed to be here," Oliver commented, shaking his head in dismay.

"Yeah, well, kind of makes two of us," Joss pointed out, alluding back to his absence and the fact that he was the son of an executioner.

She saw two figures drawing closer with three horses in tow, finding it was Henrik and Callan. Hearing the commotion, Oliver snapped out of his stunned state and spun around, barely glancing at Callan when his eyes locked on Henrik.

"Never thought I'd see *you* again," Henrik called out, stopping a short distance away.

Callan, however, was both confused and a little annoyed by the detour as he held the reins to both his horse and Drakon. The only reason he was there was so they wouldn't be separated, or worse, loose the horses and supplies to some ruffian while they were away.

Joss was about to speak up when Oliver suddenly broke out into a chuckle.

"Okay," he said, looking from Henrik to Joss. "I don't know who you all are, but I have to get going—"

"Are you serious?" the lad demanded, dropping the pony's reins and trudging forward.

"Look, I wish you all the best, but you have the wrong guy." Oliver was smiling now, trying to believe the lie. Seeing Henrik's hostility, he backed away from them all. Henrik stalked after him, but it didn't erase the knowing grin. Oliver didn't view him as a threat, knowing full well about his cleft hand.

"How about I help remind you," Henrik was saying, his gloved hands curling into fists.

"How about you back off," Oliver fired back, his off-the-shoulder attitude now taking an edge, seeing he wasn't able to leave easily.

"How about you tell us why you left in the middle of the

night," Henrik continued, coming to stand in front of him. The two men were grown, now seeing each other at eye level. "Explain why you abandoned us. Or, better yet, why you *planned* on abandoning us—"

"And what does it matter?" Oliver spoke out, his tone cold. "I'm not the guy you want."

"But you are!" Henrik growled, and for the first time Joss realized how personal the lad had taken it. He had been just as upset as her, but always remained the voice of reason. Seeing this side of him was surprising, though part of her understood it wasn't Oliver's betrayal he was acting on but also Elora's, someone else from his past who had let him down. The lad had reached his breaking point.

"Henrik, easy," Joss spoke up, coming to stand between the two of them. It was her turn to put her hand on his arm, and although he didn't meet her gaze, he held back for her.

"Yeah, Henrik. You should take it easy since you have the wrong guy," Oliver mouthed off, standing his ground to the lad he always considered weaker. "You should keep your dog on a better leash, woman," he continued, aiming his glare on Joss.

Joss pressed her lips together, feeling her anger spark. Dropping her hand from Henrik's arm, she turned to face Oliver, but not before she tightened her hand into a fist and backhanded Oliver across the face, causing a *yelp* to escape him as he staggered backwards, holding his nose.

"Enough!" Callan's voice boomed from behind, and before they could react, the prince was already standing between them, the horses left behind. "Enough with this bullshit. What's going on here?"

"He's my younger brother," Joss confessed, shaking her hand out from the hit.

Callan stared at her, putting the pieces together. "Blood related?"

Joss nodded as a heavy-breathing Oliver faced them, rubbing his jaw and wiping the blood from his nose. "Lies!" he screamed.

"Knock it off! If I want your opinion, I'll beat it out of you." Callan's sharp glare silenced him. Turning to Henrik, Callan asked, "So why are *you* so upset?"

"You don't know what his absence did to this family," the lad growled, his glare never leaving Oliver.

Oliver laughed again, as if finding the idiocy of it all amusing.

Joss eyed her brother before realizing Callan was staring directly at her. In his dark gaze, she found he had caught on. "You're the executioner of Galmoor... because of *him*," he stated, pointing to Oliver.

Joss was hesitant, unable to confirm or deny it. Denying meant she was lying; confirming meant there would be consequences.

"This is bullshit!" Oliver yelled. "I'm not an executioner!"

"You were supposed to be!" Henrik bellowed back. "It's your birthright, your responsibility! She took over because of you—"

"*So what?*" Oliver snapped, losing his composure. "What was I supposed to do, *stay?* Kill people for a living? Be killed if I didn't do the job right, like they did with Flynn?" His eyes suddenly narrowed on Joss. "Or be killed by *you*, just like Celine."

The air rushed out of her lungs, leaving her speechless. The news had reached him after all.

"Celine's dead because she was following *your* example—" Henrik lunged at him, but was caught by both Joss and Callan. While Joss held onto his arm, she realized very quickly Callan had been the one to block most of the action.

"Relax," the prince was whispering, as if soothing a temperamental steed. Henrik, however, was too busy glaring at Oliver to really listen.

"And I'm supposed to take responsibility for that?" Oliver spat back. "You two were supposed to watch her!"

"Kind of hard when people are sneaking off in the middle of the night," Henrik snarled. Joss pressed a hand against his chest to keep him back while Callan shifted away, seeing she had him under control.

"Doesn't matter whose fault it is," Callan spoke up, looking pointedly at Oliver, "You're fucked either way."

Oliver wiped more blood from his nose, his breaths heavy from anger. "You don't know what you're talking about," he tried to scoff off.

Callan smirked a little, clearly enjoying being underestimated. "If you're the last male heir, then the executioner duties fall to you. And since you've deserted those duties, you have two options: resume them while paying a heavy fine or refuse and be punished, which is usually physical and involves branding the side of the neck with a hot iron so everyone knows of your shame, if I'm not mistaken."

Oliver stared at him wide-eyed, his chest rising and falling with his labored breaths.

"But you already knew that—" Callan grinned at him "—given

how badly you tried to deny it all."

"I'm not an executioner," Oliver whispered, irritation being replaced by desperation. "I can't be one."

"I agree completely, but rules are rules," Callan shrugged. "Stay or hide; make your choice. The consequences will find you anyway."

"No," Oliver replied, panicked, looking back to Joss. "No, I'm not a Brevyn. Tell them."

Joss didn't try to reply as her hand dropped from holding Henrik back, who remained next to her without any more fighting. Oliver had already denounced her as family, but hearing it so plainly spoken... she hadn't expected that. She had imagined finding him again; thought that, yes, maybe he'd deny everything and there would be an argument. But in those daydreams, she was the one yelling, the one who was angry. They all ended in a form of reconciliation, though. This wasn't the ending she had expected to find.

"Say it!" Oliver suddenly demanded. "I'm not your brother!"

Joss's vision blurred, knowing she couldn't have him undergo those conditions. However, she couldn't deny his actions had hurt, a part of her just wanting him to take some accountability.

"But you are," Henrik replied for her, his anger more lucid than hers. "And you left us with this mess."

"I have a family," Oliver pleaded.

Those words woke her up. "*We* were your family," Joss spoke up, unable to stop herself. "I helped raise you when mom died— you and Celine—and you left us, like none of it mattered."

Oliver stared at her, as if she wasn't getting it. "I have a daughter."

And that was it; Joss knew she had lost. He had a family, children, everything she once wanted before she had to pick up their father's ax and carry out his duties as the last one left in the family. With that choice, she put down her dreams of having her own family, her own children. Children of executioners became executioners, and she couldn't do that to them. She refused to pass the burden on.

Her chest tightened, seeing how he had taken more from her than she realized. "And I don't," she replied softly, the tears showing how much it hurt, a dream killed so another could flourish.

Something shifted close to her, and that's when she felt Henrik's arm pressed next to hers, letting her know in his own way that she wasn't alone.

"Say it," Oliver persisted. "You don't have a living brother."

Joss softly shook her head at him. "The thing is, I do," she retorted, "it's just not you."

While Henrik's hand found hers, she still had to watch how Oliver's shoulders sagged in relief, how the smile appeared, how everything worked out in his favor. He didn't say thank you, didn't reply with any gesture of gratitude. He simply turned and walked off, and without looking back, he yelled out for good measure in case anyone overheard the exchange, "Stay away from me, witch! We don't need your kind here!"

Joss stared after him, her eyes blurring from the slander, wishing the news of their sister had never reached him. While she could have easily hated him right then, she didn't. He had a little one now, and that forced her to see that his actions weren't all selfish—he was just trying to protect his own. Wouldn't she do the same thing if she were in that position?

As Oliver's form grew smaller, the trees cutting into her view, Joss kept her gaze on him. She knew she wouldn't see him again; this was it, her last moment. *He's okay*, she decided to tell herself, knowing that she wouldn't have to look for him anymore. She could put that burden down now.

Callan, however, huffed out in annoyance. "Well, that was pathetic," he concluded, before his tone softened upon seeing her staring. "He's a coward. He's not deserving of being your brother."

Joss's eyes shifted to him, and with a small nod, she agreed.

Callan gave her an encouraging nod before trudging back to the horses. "We should head out before we make more friends. We're losing daylight," he called over his shoulder.

"What about your shirt?" Henrik spoke up, recalling why they had stopped in the first place.

"My wife will just have to take me as-is."

"Lucky her," Henrik mumbled.

"I heard that," Callan called back.

Joss's gaze had fallen back to the forest, even after Oliver was long gone and out of sight. With a squeeze on her hand, she found Henrik looking down at her, subtly reminding her that they needed to go. Turning away, the two made their way to the horses, Henrik letting go of her hand and draping his arm over her shoulder, squeezing her close to him as they walked. "Are you going to be okay?" he whispered.

"I should ask you the same thing." She tried to make things light-hearted, like he would have done.

"I'm better now," he admitted, though his expression showed

that he was concerned.

"Me too," Joss reassured him, adding somberly, "Now we know we have a niece."

Nellie. At least she knew her name.

"Yeah, we do," Henrik whispered back, keeping in step with her.

Making their way back to the horses, they both silently agreed that, despite their predicament, at least one generation of Brevyns had been saved.

CHAPTER EIGHT

In the past, Aric would have acted differently.

He would have been the one to close the door to the harlot's room, his mouth finding hers, practically suffocating her as the corset was unlaced and ripped off. He would have picked her up and thrown her onto the bed to give himself time to disrobe, and then he'd position himself over her and have his way.

Unfortunately, this time it was him who was pushed onto the bed, very unexpectedly and not quite as gracefully as all the girls made it out to be.

Slightly flailing, Aric landed on the bed with a bounce, Andrina already crawling on top of him with a look bordering predatory. She straddled him, and while the view was nice, he couldn't find the urge to appreciate it.

"You like how the tables have turned?" she teased him.

"Toppled, more likely," he joked.

She smiled at him, slipping the other thin strap of her dress down, both now hanging off her shoulders.

"I saw you have a new bartender," Aric commented, just before she bent down and kissed him, biting his bottom lip when he didn't kiss back.

"Is that why you're not turned on? The bartender is what did it for you?" she smirked, trying to get any kind of rise out of him.

Aric matched her look. "I'm only curious," he answered as she hovered her face over his.

"You're not being as curious as you usually are," Andrina whispered back, her blonde curls framing her face, making her his focal point.

"My apologies, milady," he teased, moving her hair out of his way, which she took as an invitation to kiss him again.

He had kissed without feeling before, even with her. He had been with prettier girls too, more accomplished women who he could very much have without losing his head to passion and romance. But this kiss, even when it meant nothing, felt... wrong. It didn't set him on fire or make the world evaporate around him. This wasn't Jocelyn while on a ledge. This wasn't what he wanted in a kiss.

If it wasn't for the sudden sounds coming from the room next door, the wall separating them right near his head, he wasn't sure how he was going to sidestep this mess.

The muffled moans and yells made his eyebrows knit together as he pulled away from her lips, only imagining what kind of passions were at play next door. He knew he could make things loud too, but these tenants were being obnoxious about it. Except, the woman involved sounded faintly familiar...

"Someone's having fun," Andrina laughed before her lips

found his ear, her teeth pulling gently on his earlobe. His skin prickled along his neck, and he fought the urge to swat her away and really start a fight.

"I guess they have a lot of stress to work out," he commented, causing Andrina to laugh, which almost deafened him by how close she was. "Has anything else changed while I've been gone?" he asked.

Andrina was quiet, too consumed in her task. "Not really," the harlot finally admitted.

"Has our lost prince returned yet?" he tried again.

There was a slight chuckle. "Of course not. His wife still goes to the cathedral every day to pray for him and light a candle but has nothing to show for it." She sucked a little harder, causing Aric to grimace. If it had been a certain someone else, his reaction would have been much different.

"Still prays, huh?" he asked, remembering that insignificant detail.

"Every day she spends a couple of hours with God, and then spends the rest of her days by the king's bedside. There are rumors, but between you and me, she doesn't look like a woman who has been satisfied in a while."

"Do you blame her?" Aric questioned, gritting his teeth when her tongue traced the outline of his ear. "Her husband's been missing and will be declared dead soon."

"I guess Muriel Ronen isn't meant to be queen then."

Something about the tone in that statement was a little too heartless, especially since he knew how alive Callan Ronen was. In response, Aric placed his hands on her hips, ready to rotate her off when she suddenly lifted her torso up, sitting heavily on him. The way her eyes glazed over, he found he had invited the wrong kind of attention.

Seeing she was going for his shirt, he grabbed both her wrists so she wouldn't rip it off him. He didn't want her seeing his stitches, reminders of the last time he was disrobed in front of a woman, one he couldn't stop thinking about. They were intimate to him, something he didn't want to share with anyone else except with the one person who had carefully put them in place. A small part of him didn't want to share her either.

"What are you doing?" Andrina asked, breathlessly.

"I'm sorry, I'm just too tired." It wasn't a lie; it had been a very exhausting trip.

"You're never tired," Andrina rebutted, arching an eyebrow as she sat up a little more.

Touché, Aric thought, his hands straying from her hips and resting on his chest. "I'll pay you anyway if I can just use your bed for an hour. I need the rest."

She stared at him. In all honesty, he should have seen the slap coming a mile away. If only he hadn't been lying down, causing his eyes to partially close. Despite the ruckus next door, exhaustion was setting in.

The slap, however, was an instant wake up call.

"The hell are you doing here, then?" she demanded, scrambling off his lap. Her movements caused the bed to move, bouncing him along as he rubbed his jaw. "Who is she?!"

An executioner. "No one," he lied, sitting up.

"Where did you meet her?"

In the countryside, unfortunately. "Nowhere."

"Are you in love with her?"

Helplessly. "Who could I be in love with if there's no one?"

"Don't answer me with a question!" she spat, hands on her hips while standing her ground, the neighbors hollering away in the background, which was becoming increasingly annoying given how Aric and Andrina stared at each other.

"I'm tired," Aric tried again. "I've had a long journey with an exceedingly long job request, and all I need is an hour."

She glared at him, and for a long moment they stared each other down. Finally, she broke, huffing out in a sigh as she turned to face the dresser and mirror, her reflection angry and downcast. "Fine. Have it," she receded.

He sat up on the edge of the bed, curious as to why she was acting like this. Had she wanted something more? The thought never crossed his mind.

"I'm sorry if I offended you," Aric spoke up, offering to mend their friendship at least.

She hummed to herself, her eyes down, her hands seeming to fiddle in front of her. "I actually don't care who you're with. I missed you and it got the better of me. I normally don't have regulars who are like you."

Aric didn't stop himself from feeling flattered as she turned a little to face him, his knee resting on the bed.

"If it was someone, what would she be like?" she mused, looking at him through the mirror.

He smirked at her. *Oh, no you don't,* he thought, refusing to play that game. "Most likely a harlot," he threw back, because at one point in his life, it would have been the truth.

Andrina looked up in thought, and he could see her beautiful face light up in a soft smile. "I imagine she'd be plain, for my own amusement," she teased.

Anyway, Aric thought, already bored with the topic. He bent over, pulling his boot off.

"Maybe a little well built, given she'd have to cut her own firewood."

Aric paused, an eyebrow raised as he looked at Andrina's smiling reflection.

"Plain girls would have to cut their own," she shrugged before running her fingers through her golden curls like a hairbrush. "She definitely wouldn't have my hair. It would be darker—"

Aric gave her a look but resumed taking his boot off, mindful of the knife he kept hidden.

The harlot was looking at her own reflection now, her hand gracing her neck. "I could see no other man wanting her, which is why you took it upon yourself with the task. That's why I like you; you see people no one else does."

Aric's actions were fluid as he moved the boots away and pulled his hood off, running his hands through his hair. What she didn't see was how she gained his attention, how attuned he was to her movements, her words. Even the noises next door had fallen deaf to him.

Thinking he was ignoring her, she slowly opened the top drawer, her hand dipping in just before she shut it quietly. Then she started fiddling with the top of her corset, as if it needed adjusting. Shaking her head, she acted like she was shaking out her hair, refreshing herself.

Another bent scream pierced the air through the wall behind him, their bed already involved as it squeaked along in rhythm. Aric bent over, resting his elbows on his knees while rubbing his hands, wishing the two would finish already.

"I thought you were going to bed?" Andrina reminded him, eyeing him as she turned around.

With his jaw clenched, he stared the harlot down as she strolled over to him, a seductive look plastered on her face that she had mastered over the years. Taking a deep breath, he bowed his head, and she ran her hands through his hair, pressing her body against his forehead. He breathed her in, the faint rosewater scent invading his nostrils as he closed his eyes. *I'll miss this,* he thought, unable to lie to himself.

"You know," she said in a hushed voice. "You always come back to me."

Aric didn't think as he lifted his hands to her hips again, feeling the heat of her skin through her thin dress. He was too busy listening to her voice, fixated on where her hands were.

"That must say something." Her fingers continued to brush through his long hair, moving it from his face.

Aric took another deep breath, waiting.

"I'm all you have left," she continued, and that's when he felt one of her hands disappear.

As he held onto her body, he noticed the tension, the slight contraction of her body as she lifted her arm. The movement was quick as she raised her arm before slamming it down, sudden and violent, but not before her arm was caught by Aric's hand, which shot up to stop her. He had been studying her body, feeling for it, knowing the attack was coming. It was like watching a snake as it prepared to strike.

Throwing his head back, he was met with her stunned but angry face and the small dagger glinting in the gaslight.

Moving his ankle behind hers, he shoved her backwards, tripping her. She fell to the ground as he stood up, still holding her arm. The dagger remained tight in her fist, so he dug his thumbnails into the inside of her forearm, causing her grasp to falter and the blade to fall to the ground. Without warning, she threw her foot into his stomach, kicking him and sending him backwards a couple steps as the air snapped out of his lungs.

Scrambling to her feet, Andrina snatched the blade and held it out between them, her eyes wild, her hair a mess.

"So that was the plan," Aric smiled a little while holding his stomach. "Seduce me, stab me, call it a day."

Andrina was breathing hard, but it didn't stop the sly smile from forming. "You were always worth more dead than alive. We both know it."

"True, but you didn't have to say it," he replied, a little disgusted.

She lunged at him, and he flung himself to the side, finding himself cornered between the door and the wall where the lovers had yet to break pace.

"You must have been paid handsomely for this," Aric commented. The knife in his boot would be no help as he watched her reach down and take it out.

Shit, she remembers where I keep them, he growled in thought as she grasped both blades in either hand.

"You have no idea," she smiled, as if she had been given the world with only Aric standing in the way of receiving it.

"And here I thought you were caring about me," he reminded her. "Or was that jealous bit a part of the act?"

"Does it matter?" she asked before lunging at him, slashing one of the blades in front of her and causing his back to hit the door, dodging it.

"Answering a question with a question." He tsked at her. "Hypocrite."

She lunged at him again, but this time he hit her arm, causing her to lose one of the blades. She screamed in pain, stabbing into the air as she swung her arm and missed. Grabbing her other arm, he held her in front of him, but was temporarily blinded when she rammed her forehead into his nose, causing his eyes to instantly water as blood filled his nostrils. Groaning through gritted teeth, he pushed her backwards onto the bed to get rid of her, snatching the blade from the ground, which was the knife she had taken from his boot.

Standing up, he positioned himself back in front of the door as he wiped the blood trailing to his lips while Andrina scrambled off the bed. He couldn't be mad she had gotten him. It was his own fault; he had taught her that move, back when he thought she could use the help in case a client got a little too rowdy.

She charged at him, and out of reflex, he blocked her wrist again and stabbed her with the knife, hitting its mark right into her side. She screamed as the blade sunk in. Staggering back, she swung her arm and sliced at his abdomen, causing him to growl when the blade cut through his shirt and lightly met his skin. In pain and enraged, Andrina charged again, this time a hand on his throat, the knife raised in the air to strike him.

He found the handle of the blade stuck in her side, and begrudgingly he pulled it out and stabbed her again with it, twisting the handle. Her hands froze in place as she screamed, which he covered with his other hand so no one would hear her. By the sound of the neighbors, nothing could seem to interfere with their activities.

Andrina stared at him, panting into his palm and fingers. The tears were streaming now, and as he looked at her with anticipation, he knew he had won when her knife slipped from her grip and landed on the floor.

Removing his hand, Aric held her as her body became heavy. Leaning back against the door for support, he was a little sorry things had to end this way.

Blood formed at the corners of her mouth. "Why her?" she whispered, and in her gaze he saw the hurt that wasn't coming from the knife.

So, it wasn't an act, he thought.

Only one person would have known about Jocelyn and what she meant to him; someone who had caught on to his feelings from the very beginning.

Ah, there it is: leverage. It was back at Jocelyn and Henrik's cottage, when the Mask found him and Aric had slipped up. *But fair warning, villain to villain: don't make yourself too comfortable here. You may find yourself complicating things.*

The bastard had been right.

"I have my reasons," he replied, also panting as he held Andrina in place.

"She's a deathsman, Aric," Andrina hissed. "Nobody wants her."

"*I* want her." The words matched his growl.

"So, I was right," she spat angrily, spitting blood on him.

Aric narrowed his gaze. "Except it's not because I saw her when no one else did," he confessed. "I love her because she saw *me.*"

And she hasn't tried killing me, you crazy bitch, he seethed inside, reaching down to pull the knife out of her again, causing Andrina to shriek.

"Who paid you?" he tried again, leveling his gaze at her.

Breathing heavily, Andrina forced a smile, her teeth smeared with blood. She leaned in and kissed Aric on the lips. Pulling back, her smile remained. "Good luck," she crooned. "You're going to need it."

Accepting her choice, Aric made sure it was a quick death by bringing the blade up and slicing her throat, holding her neck as her head fell back and the blood drained down her chest and corset. He awkwardly lifted her into his arms as her body twitched, her mouth gaped open as her eyes rolled back into her skull. Placing her gently on the bed, he stayed by her side until the twitching subsided.

As he sat watching, he had to admit to himself that it was the betrayal he reacted to, not quite the mercy of ending her suffering. If he wanted to be honest with himself, Andrina was the harlot he would have ended up with, if he was to end up with someone.

They had known each other far longer than anyone else, had been intimate and physical in ways they hadn't been with others, and yet Andrina had turned so easily against him. For the money or jealousy, it was a toss-up which had sent her over the edge.

Jocelyn, however, had done the opposite. She was genuine and had no ulterior motives, which made him uncomfortable at first. All his relationships, professional and physical, came at a price, but she had never expected anything. Jocelyn had opened her home up to him, stitched him back together, and yet never asked for anything in return. Even when he pushed her off that ledge and threatened her with the crossbow twice, she didn't act or treat him the way Andrina had, though he rightfully deserved it. Jocelyn had every cause to hate him more—and the world, for that matter— and yet she was the one who chose to remain kind.

I don't deserve you, he thought, thinking of her while Andrina bled out onto the bed, her body lax. Jocelyn would have known how to help her, to save her life. Aric had only thought about taking it.

Breathing out harshly, he could hear the neighbors still going at it as he remained sitting on the bed, putting his boots back on and trying to think things through. *It had to have been the Mask*, his mind was pounding, giving him a headache. *But how? When?*

The moans and sharp cries were replaced with foul words now. Aric couldn't help burying his head in his hands, exhaustion sitting so deep inside that he almost thought he might have to push Andrina aside and sleep off the disappointment. At least his nose had stopped bleeding.

But then the moans changed, becoming higher as the pace

began to quicken as the end was coming, and that's when Aric's body instantly tightened. Slowly lifting his head up out of his hands, he turned his hard gaze to the wall. That voice, the pitch… he knew exactly who that woman was. He knew because he too had been the reason behind them, hearing the same tone just before he sent her over the edge. He had always made sure to hear it, knowing he was doing things right.

He knew because that woman in the next room was none other than Andrina.

CHAPTER NINE

Keep him preoccupied, Muriel told herself. *It's the only way to keep Callan alive.*

With nothing nice to say, the conversation was minimal as Muriel and Davien made their way out to the city streets, passing the guards at the entrance of the wall. The sun was overhead now, morning long gone. Muriel shielded her eyes with her hand and glanced up at the battlements. A sense of longing overcame her as she moved underneath the portcullis and ventured into the bustling city street, having to leave her first plan behind.

Her second plan, which she admitted wasn't as romantic as the first, was simply to keep Davien distracted. It was obvious he was with her for a reason, assuming Callan would try to reach out to her once he was back behind the walls. That was made clear as he gazed over the crowds, knowing deep down he was looking for a different type of threat, one that would take his chance of holding the crown. Muriel was simply a pawn to him, and she hated herself for having to play into his scheme. *But two can play this game*, she reminded herself, thinking that maybe she could help Callan by keeping Davien detained. His goons would be keeping a lookout, but maybe she could stall him somehow. Maybe she could get in his way.

As they moved away from the entrance, Muriel slowly came to a stop, realizing she missed something.

"What are you waiting for?" Davien asked impatiently, immediately stopping with her, which was unnerving. She thought he was keeping his eyes on their surroundings, yet he was attuned to her every step, every look.

"Aren't we taking guards with us?" she asked pointedly. Even with her ladies-in-waiting present, a handful of guards always accompanied them as protection. It was so routine that she often forgot about them—until now when their absence was louder than the street vendors.

"We don't need guards," he scoffed, flicking his wrist in the direction of the cathedral, telling her to keep moving.

Pressing her lips together, Muriel begrudgingly moved forward with Davien keeping step right next to her. By how close he was, she easily viewed him as a jailer taking her back to her cell.

The morning vendors were in full swing, the noises and smells bearing down on the streets as Muriel followed the path to the cathedral. In between the buildings, she caught glimpses of the cathedral's tall peaks, wishing it were closer to the castle. The lack of communication yet closeness of having Davien around was making her nervous, especially since at any moment she anticipated seeing Callan. Every hood, every back turned—it was always *almost* him, until it wasn't. Only a couple of times did she glance at Davien sideways, finding he too was keeping an eye out.

Then she saw them: the patrolling guards. At least, that's what she thought they were, until she noticed they were meandering around, keeping their distance despite following where she and Davien were traveling. *That's why we don't need guards*, she thought in disgust. *They're already here.*

She wondered if this was normal when Davien left the castle, the guards keeping a distant watch instead of remaining by his side like they did with her. Or had Davien upped the patrols, some of them in his favor and also keeping an eye out for Callan?

Despite the observation, as well as dodging other pedestrians and peddlers trying to grab anyone's attention, Muriel kept quietly searching. She wondered what Callan would look like now, how much he had changed. She knew he'd always look like his father, but she wondered if his eyes would still be the same—would they be as expressive and curious as before, or hard and detached like his brothers? Callan's eyes were darker in color, but the other two heirs were darker in spirit. Even Eiden, who was the more laid back of the princes, couldn't hide the lack of empathy in his gaze.

The apprehension was settling in as Muriel rounded a corner and the cathedral came into full view, an old structure nestled against the city life. Davien remained at her elbow, scouting the area as those who noticed the two royals bowed in respect, muttering "Your Highnesses" as they went. Some pretended not to notice them, while others didn't pretend at all and blatantly kept quiet. Muriel would have thought it a concern if it hadn't been for the guards sprawled out in the area.

As they advanced closer, the ancient arches of the stained-glass windows came into view, and taking the steps, Davien moved forward enough to open the door, ushering her in.

Hearing the echo of the door closing, Muriel faced the nave, the rows of bench seats lining the aisle as the stone buttresses arched overhead. The stained-glass cast shadows of color across the floor as she moved quietly forward, the sound of her footsteps floating up into the air. A few visitors were already inside, scattered across the pews to keep their distance from each other as they prayed.

Reaching the crossing, Muriel made a left, coming face-to-face with the tiered rows of candlelight, which sat underneath a stained-glass window of a rose. Many came to light a candle to remember a loved one, to sympathize in moments of grief, or to hope in bringing a loved one back either from sickness or war. Sometimes the candle was lit in times of victory or in the birth of a child, the light flickering in thanks, and sometimes it was as simple as just being filled with faith. These were all symbols of the rose, and the small votive candles were a glowing reminder that all these reasons—good or bad—were universal, that no one was alone in their prayers.

However, the rose was also a sign of persistence, and that's what Muriel lit her candle for. No matter the obstacle, Callan would come home.

A few of the candles were lit, flickering here and there, while the rest remained dark. The solitude was deafening as Muriel and Davien approached. Thinking he would have stepped up to the candles with her, Davien came to an immediate halt as if the candles themselves were a threat. When she looked at him in wonder, she found his face was bent into a disgusted expression, believing the whole procedure irrelevant, a complete waste of time. He only ever stepped foot in the cathedral for royal ceremonies, and it was evident by his demeanor that whatever faith he had wasn't religious based.

Feeling a little offended but not entirely surprised, Muriel continued on, picking up one of the unlit candles and holding it upside down over another candle's flame. Once the candle was lit, she put it back in place and then closed her eyes, reciting the same prayer she always did, hoping the candle's light would help the prayer's longevity.

"Feel better now?"

Muriel pressed her lips together, ignoring Davien's comment behind her. She heard him creep forward, his presence overshadowing hers as he came to stand next to her.

"Are you going to continue with this little ritual after we're married?"

Muriel's eyes snapped open. "I'll never marry you—"

"But you will," Davien chuckled. "And if you keep being stubborn, I'm sure my men can help persuade you."

The heat stretched across her neck, sweat forming between her shoulder blades as the anger surfaced. "You're always full of threats, aren't you?" she hissed back. "First, it was sending me off to fend for myself, then it was turning me out onto the streets like a harlot. Now, it's to become entertainment for those brutes you call 'men.' What next, Davien? You'll chain me to a wall and flog me into submission?"

He was quick when he snatched her wrist, pulling her into him and causing her wide eyes to stare directly into his dark gaze.

"If that's what it takes to break your spirit, then so be it," he snarled back. "You will be mine. I don't give a shit about what I have to do to accomplish it—break your spirit, mutilate your body—you will be *mine*. No matter what happens, princess, I will win. And very soon, it will be my name you scream, even if it's from all the pain."

Muriel's hands shook as she yanked her wrist free, staggering backwards. She saw the door to the side leading out to the back garden. Seeing it as an escape, she darted for it, her dress rustling around her as she ran, unaware that Davien was still keeping his eyes on her.

CHAPTER TEN

Aselian was larger than any city Joss or Henrik had ever seen. The realm stretched for miles, wrapping around the side of a lake before advancing towards the hills, extending into farmlands in all directions. The lake was fed by the mountains peeking in the distance, which in turn fed the river they had followed through the canyon of rocky cliffs. Upon making the last turn, the valley opened, and there, sprawled inside, was Aselian.

Joss couldn't keep her eyes off it, soaking it all in as they followed Callan at a walking pace, trying not to look too hurried as they passed more travelers who were both coming and going. Keeping a low profile, they made sure their hoods were drawn up while paying close attention to those they passed. However, once the kingdom came into view, Joss temporarily forgot her surroundings. This was where all the rules were made, where her family had sent all their pardons that were denied. This was where Callan belonged, what he had come to fight for and take back, a realm he called home.

This was also Aric's home, a place where he too belonged.

Swallowing hard, her hands tightened on the reins which she had to stretch out, hoping no one would notice. While the interaction with Oliver had subdued her, thinking of Aric perked her up, a reaction she wasn't used to.

After seeing the kingdom come into view, Callan bolted towards it. They had ridden in a fervor, forgetting the travelers they were trying to blend in with, until they began to pass the farmland and enter the outskirts of civilization. Reality weighed heavily on him, and Callan brought his horse down to a trot and then eventually a walk. Henrik and Joss followed suit, coming to ride on either side of him. Both noticed how apprehensive he was, torn between hurrying and being patient. He had been waiting for this moment, but given the threat the previous day in Raspshire, he needed a plan, something he could control, especially since everything had been so out of control those nearly five years.

Now, as Joss was stretching out her hands, Callan was busy explaining Aselian's layouts. There were the battlements around the castle itself, while the rest of the town had a similar wall that stretched to the port, sitting at the rim of the lake. Farther down was the castle, built right up onto the lake and so tall that it mirrored the peaks in the distance, which Joss assumed would be beautiful in the winter, only a short couple of months away. She imagined the whole place turning into a winter fairytale, the white and blue of the snowfall being a magical contrast to the beige stones and reddish-brown and light mint green roofs of the kingdom.

"You still light torches?" she heard Henrik asking, her eyes automatically falling to the wall and battlements. While they weren't lit, she could see where the old light system was in place, torches lit by hand. Part of her hoped she'd be able to see it at night, witnessing the ethereal touch the firelight would cast, especially against the lake.

"There's a lot to power when it comes to the castle," Callan answered. "It even has its own watermill, just on the other side against the lake."

Joss nodded in understanding, unable to pull her gaze from the sight, committing it all to memory.

"A copper mine is to the east of us," Callan continued, noticing how both Joss and Henrik were admiring the tops of the structures, never seeing those types of colors on buildings before. "We used it to make the roofs. Over the centuries, the copper started to turn green with age. You can tell which are newer by the shade of color the roof is."

Joss imagined all the rooftops being copper against the lake and forest. While it would have been lovely, she found the mixture of copper and mint alluring.

"And you actually *live* here?" Henrik was nodding to the castle, unable to fathom that one family could have such a massive structure all to themselves.

Callan grinned. "Born and raised." He then pointed to a couple of the castle's towers. "Those are the bell towers. You can't see the bells from this angle, but that's what will tell everyone I'm home."

"Not the cathedral?" Henrik asked, comparing the layout to Galmoor. The only bell the canal town had was the church, ringing for all occasions.

"It'll be rung too. However, the castle's bell towers are for the royal family, or for a serious situation, such as a war or a warning of some kind. We've seen peace for many years, so they're really only used for weddings, births, and deaths, just like the cathedral. The last time I heard each toll was on the day I was married."

While it was a common thought, no one voiced that both bells would also announce the death of the king, each hoping it would be a sound they wouldn't have to hear.

"It's... remarkable," Henrik finally breathed out in awe.

Joss agreed. The way the castle rose into the sky was magnificent, its structure a work of art. The towers with their sweeping gold and burgundy flags, the colors of Aselian; the way the stone was laid and cut, creating grandiose arches and balconies—it was mesmerizing.

"You're being awfully quiet."

Joss brought her attention to Callan, who was staring right at her, a soft smirk on his face. "Just admiring it all," she confessed.

"Well, once this is all over, I'll give you both a proper tour. For now, we need to find a way to get into the castle."

"So, announcing yourself at the gate isn't the plan," Henrik teased.

Joss smiled despite herself. That had been Aric's joke, back at the tavern in Greywall, back when she had confessed more to him than she meant to.

"As I said before, we need to assess the situation first," Callan replied, remembering the joke vividly and still not finding it funny. "We'll need to get rid of the horses first. It's better to stay on foot once we're inside, easier to maneuver. If all else fails, we can take the tunnels."

"Tunnels?" Henrik asked, and even Joss looked at the prince in curiosity.

"Centuries ago, a group of citizens built tunnels underneath the city to meet and plot in secret. They wanted to overthrow the royal family, establish themselves as rulers, but beyond that they had no plans. They just wanted the power. When they were finally caught, the king decided to give them one chance to redeem themselves. They would fight him, prove if they were warriors enough to handle the throne. He figured if he could show the people how ridiculous they were, then maybe he'd squash any future uprisings."

"I'm assuming it worked," Henrik commented.

Callan smirked. "It's said some barely handled a sword well. He made a mockery of them. Kings are looked upon as someone who not only rules but defends his people. They can't believe that you're weak."

Joss noticed the change in tone, seeing he was talking about himself.

"Afterwards, the rules of Mors Exitus were created. The king figured it would be better to see the threat coming than deal with conspiracies."

A fight to the death, Joss thought, remembering how Callan explained it over the campfire. Anyone could challenge the king for the throne, or have someone fight in their stead, but the only one left alive was hailed as king. Even if someone conceded early, they would be put to death and the victor would be crowned. The only rule was that two witnesses had to be present.

"And the tunnels?" Henrik's attention was fully invested,

which made Joss smile a little, knowing the inquisitive part of him was feasting on the story.

"They're old, and parts of them have collapsed due to age, but until I had left, there were a few still usable. They've been given the nickname Traitor's Alley."

"And you still know the entrances?" Joss asked, wondering how intact his memory was.

By the look he gave her, his memory remained sharp. "I know them well," he said simply. "I was young once and about as mischievous as my brothers."

Joss nodded in understanding but didn't reply, watching instead as Callan regained his courage and pressed his legs into the side of the bay gelding, pushing him back into a gallop.

Henrik followed suit on the pony, and as Joss was about to follow on Drakon, she noticed in the far distance the charcoal grey clouds. The castle had taken all her attention, causing the storm clouds to go unnoticed. Now she saw them, her attention only pulled away when Drakon snorted impatiently as the other two were leaving them behind. Hastily, she followed, the dark horse gaining the distance back until they were behind Henrik again. Deep down, she hoped the storm wasn't an omen for what was to come.

The city wall was tall in its own right; guards meandering on its battlements forced the three to sink back into their hoods to hide their identity. Bringing the horses back down to a walk, the three journeyed past the gates along with some other travelers, riding underneath the portcullis that looked like dragon's teeth suspended above them. The guards said nothing, eyeing them but not recognizing the prince who had returned home. By how low Callan wore his hood, he was making sure of it, not wanting the attention in case the guards were untrustworthy.

Taking a deep breath, Joss tried to focus on keeping up despite her attention being pulled in all directions. The buildings here were higher and cleaner than home, adorned with stone carvings that made the doorways and windows elegant.

The only thing making her nervous was the people. The crowds, the vendors—it was all deja'vu to Raspshire, and given how they had left the town, every hooded figure made her heart jump. While she searched for anyone wearing a mask or following them, she also kept an eye out for a crossbow, strands of long blond hair falling over the shoulders, and a walk only an assassin seemed to carry.

Joss knew the others were keeping an eye out for the same types of individuals—except for Aric, she already assumed—by how they too were looking, their heads on a swivel. Occasional-ly, she'd look up at the balconies overhead like they had done in Raspshire, but unlike the smaller town, the balconies above had an abundance of flowers and foliage hanging off the windowsills, not just roses. Full grown ferns sat alongside an array of colorful flow-ers while vines hung down from others, some reaching the next balcony below them. When she finally brought her gaze down, she found Callan had turned to instruct them on where they were heading. He smiled at her, amused by their reactions since Henrik was doing the same thing.

Nodding to the right, he turned back around, his cue that he had found his destination. Following him through the crowds, the three dismounted in front of a stable. Finding a few vacant stalls, they paid the stable keeper with the rest of the coins they had to keep both horses and tack safe from prying hands.

Unsaddling her horse and stashing the saddle and bags in the corner of the stall, Joss fitted the ax underneath her cloak. With the blade hidden in the leather cover, she kept it underneath her arm while her cloak hid the rest of it, making it a little less obvious than if she outright carried it. While she couldn't hide the weapon completely given how wide the blade was, she knew that in passing no one would really notice; at least, not at a first glance.

Patting Drakon farewell, she moved to where Bluebelle was being kept next to him. "Don't forget the revolver," she whispered to Henrik, who nodded before digging the weapon out of the bag he too had stashed away in the stall.

"Maybe you should keep it," he suggested, standing back up. "I've never been good with these."

Understanding, Joss took the gun from him and stuffed it in the waistband of her pants like she saw men always do, keeping it on the other side of where she had her ax. Given that Henrik had his knife and Callan still kept her small pistol snug in his boot, she needed a handier weapon. The ax was effective, but not like a revolver or pistol, or Henrik's knife-throwing skills.

"Ready?"

Both turned to find Callan outside of the stall, looking in at them as he leaned against the half-wall. Joss glanced over at his horse, finding he was already put away and happily munching on hay.

"When this is all over, I'll have them sent for and moved to the royal stables," Callan reassured them.

"Even yours?" Joss asked, wondering what would happen to the steed who had made the long trip with them. She wondered if he would bother offering to give it back to the drunk he stole it from back in Galmoor.

"Oh, I'm keeping him," Callan smiled. "That horse deserves a good rest after everything I put him through. I'll make sure he gets the care he deserves."

Joss smiled back as she and Henrik ventured out of the stall, though not before Henrik said his goodbyes to the pony with another rub and "be good" lecture.

Leaving the stables behind, Joss and Henrik followed Callan down the congested street.

"So now where to?" Henrik asked, staying right by Joss's side while Callan stayed a step ahead.

"We'll head to the cathedral," Callan stated over his shoulder. "One of the tunnels starts in the chapter house."

Joss and Henrik exchanged glances, not sure of what he was talking about. Society never allowed them inside a church, so anything associated with one was a foreign topic.

Joss moved her arm a little, gripping the handle of the ax through her cloak so she could carry it better. The revolver felt out of place where it sat in her waistband, but it was better than not having it at all.

"And it'll take us to the castle?" Henrik was asking as they dodged a street vendor, working themselves around a group of standing pedestrians who were waiting to get a piece of the goods.

"It's one of the main tunnels," Callan explained as he came

up to the end of the street which was attached to another one. He made sure to keep the title of Traitor's Alley quiet in case someone overheard. "It's a straight shot to the castle, which ends up on the other side of the castle wall. Perfect for us. A few tunnels connect to it, but we won't have to deal with those."

"What about lighting?" Henrik asked, trying to know every angle so there would be fewer surprises to encounter.

"Last I knew, the lighting still worked. They hooked up a string of lights from a watermill powering that section of town. As long as the waterwheel is turning, the tunnel will have available light."

"And no one else uses these tunnels?" Joss asked, beating Henrik to the question.

She could hear the grin in Callan's tone. "The tunnels are so old many have forgotten about them. I'm sure some still use them, but not enough to be our problem. We'll be in and out before that happens."

Joss and Henrik both hoped he was right as they arrived at the junction between streets. Callan was about to cross when he stopped suddenly, causing Henrik to run into him. With a curse, the lad stepped quickly back, apologizing.

Callan, however, didn't move.

"What's wrong?" Henrik was asking as Joss moved closer to Callan, glancing at his face. The shock was there, the bewilderment as he stared. Following his line of sight, she saw the woman he was staring at. Her violet cloak and mauve dress were much richer compared to those around her, and her dark, olive skin was complemented by her thick, black hair that was elegantly braided down her back. She was beautiful, which was also a compliment that applied to the man who walked with her, equally regal but with a harshness to him that mimicked the lost prince who was staring at them.

Joss realized who it was, even before the name escaped Callan's lips.

"Muriel."

CHAPTER ELEVEN

There was something ghostly about hearing the voice of a woman whose dead body was laying just a couple of feet away.

Aric shuddered, feeling dirty at the prospect. He was curious about the room next door, but was too busy rummaging through the dresser, needing to find any clues. His gut told him it was the Mask, but he needed confirmation. Unfortunately, nothing helped him. The room was merely a stage, the harlots being the performers.

Slamming the last dresser drawer, Aric stood up and looked at the wall, finding the noises were persisting as if the whole scenario was being repeated. Making his way back to the door with knife in hand, he took one last look at the room. He had checked under the bed, the mattresses, behind the dresser. He searched through Andrina's wardrobe and still came up empty handed. Glancing at her one last time, he pulled his hood on and turned the doorknob, peering through the crack in the door. Finding the hall was clear—save for a few other noisy tenants—Aric slipped out of the room, closing the door behind him.

He made his way to the next room, hearing the muffled sounds he had grown to despise from behind the door. Trying the door-knob, he found it was locked. Odd, given that the brothel tended to have a no-lock policy to protect their girls from unruly payees. Harlots brought in money, so losing one also meant losing an employee, something not easily replaceable.

Aric looked from one end of the hall to the other, and before he could tell himself otherwise, he kicked the door, aiming for above the doorknob. The door cracked open, wood splintering as it swung open, slamming into the wall. There were no screams as he gripped the knife harder and charged in, no break in rhythm as he peered into the room and found... nothing.

Closing the door quickly behind him, Aric found the bed was empty, made, and unused while the gaslamp sizzled overhead with light. The noises, much louder though still slightly muffled, were coming in the direction of the dresser facing him, backing up to the wall that separated the room from the one he was just in. On top of the dresser was a large wooden box, a metal horn-shaped object rising from it, the sound coming from within its piping. A closer inspection showed a wax-looking cylinder spinning in the center of it, creating the noises.

A phonograph, he remembered someone once calling it. The ability to record music, voices, any kind of sound. The problem was that these weren't prevalent in Aselian. This was a creation of Bellumortis, a far-off kingdom that loved its technology about as much as it loved terrifying anyone in their way. Their king was reckless, merciless; a kingdom everyone side-stepped, not wanting to make enemies or allies of. They were advanced not only in technology but warfare, and it was common knowledge that anyone who challenged Bellumortis would be doomed, hence the reason Aselian stayed as far away as possible. Even when gifts were brought to buy allegiances, Aselian always declined, not wanting to owe a debt to a kingdom that was brutal, especially to its own people.

That's why seeing the phonograph was a little alarming. This was a Bellumortis contraption, something leaked out—or planted, given how conniving they were—to show the world their advancements. Aric only knew of them because a couple of his targets had been owners of these devices, paying heavily for something the king of Aselian didn't even have, an allegiance bought behind closed doors. It had boosted their self-esteem, giving them God-complexes until Aric came along and made them bleed like mortals. The fact that a phonograph was in a brothel meant someone very wealthy or highly connected was frequenting the place often.

Or royal, Aric thought as he found a switch and pressed it down, which instantly killed the sound, making the room deafeningly quiet. A pang hit his chest as if he had killed Andrina twice, which he had to brush off so he could focus. He searched the dresser like he had done with the other one. He even looked through the phonograph, searching for any clues left behind by the owner.

Finding nothing, he went to the bed, pulled off the blankets, and checked the mattress. With a huff of irritation, he bent down on his knees and looked under, finding nothing except for a floorboard sticking slightly up.

Getting up, he tried to move to the bed, only to find it stuck. Confused, Aric pushed and prodded, trying to scoot the bed to the side to find that it wouldn't budge. In an act of desperation, Aric gritted his teeth as he pulled the bed forward, and as suddenly as it happened, he heard a click and then the end of the bed lifted upward. Backing out of the way, he watched in surprise as the bed folded back, becoming parallel with the wall.

Looking down, he found latches securing the legs of the bed in place. And there, towards the end of where the foot of the bed had been, was the lifted floorboard. He could now see it was a handle to a sliding door, hidden by the length of the bed.

Moving around to the side, he bent down and moved the handle, sliding the hidden door back until he was met with a narrow staircase that spiraled downward. He had never seen a stairwell downstairs like this, which means it must have been hidden behind the walls in between the two bars.

Clever, he silently applauded. Finding nothing to take with him to light the way, he took a couple of breaths and began his journey downward. The cascading light from the gaslamp overhead slowly disappeared as he moved deeper into the stairwell. It was when he suddenly stepped on something, causing the door to slide shut above him and hearing the *thunk* of the bed as it latched back in place, that Aric wondered if maybe he should have thought this through better.

CHAPTER TWELVE

The sun blinded Muriel as she escaped from the alcove in the cathedral, sprinting into the open air with no sense of where she was going. She just had to get away from him, no matter where it led her.

At first everything went white until she shielded her eyes, blinking away the glare of the afternoon sunlight. The smell of roses overtook her as she slowed her jog to a brisk walk, never stopping as Davien's words continued to follow her. She felt the layers of her dress, the heavy silks pressing against her, the corset constricting against her ribcage. The cloak didn't help either, hanging on her like a weight. She needed to get out of the sun, out of the city, to be free of this ridiculous dress! It wasn't until she came to the end of the stone structure that she finally slowed her pace to a stop.

Breathing heavily, Muriel continued to shield her eyes as she looked at the garden. It was modest in size compared to the gardens behind the castle's walls, but it was still enclosed by large walls towering over the greenery, protecting it from the trampling of city life. The chapter house was on the other side of the cathedral, its high stained-glass windows being a small replica of its predecessor. And before her, covering the grounds were pathways enclosed by rose bushes.

These rose bushes were large and overgrown, already rising well over her own height. The placement of the bushes created a maze of intricate walkways, allowing peaceful and private meanderings for those who needed it. A couple of monks were attending to the plants, plucking the wilted petals away while their hoods shielded their faces from the sun. Used to visitors, they didn't turn her way when she began to walk towards one of the walkways. When Muriel looked behind her, she found that Davien hadn't followed.

Her heart was still racing as she pursued the pathway that wound around the roses, the bushes so dense that walking down the path was like walking down a hallway, fragranced flowers in place of walls. The roses themselves were all distinct colors—reds, oranges, purples, whites, solids, and swirls—and Muriel could feel Davien and his threat slipping from her mind, replaced by a memory she kept close to her chest.

She and Callan used to meet in this garden. They used to walk these paths, at first as childhood friends, then as flirting teenagers. Their love story had bloomed here, cultivated and attended to with as much tenderness as the rose garden itself. Of course, the guards had seen them, but no one knew to what extent their friendship had deepened until it was too late for anyone to intervene.

Muriel followed the pathway around a bend, knowing exactly

the area they first held hands, where they shared their first kiss. This garden held all their secrets, and walking these paths was like walking down countless memories that filled her with both happiness and heartache. Even when Callan couldn't be around, pulled to training or endless meetings, he always managed to leave her notes. They were always on thin strips of paper, rolled tightly into a secret and left for only her to find, even in the garden. Somehow, he always knew which flower to hide them in, paying so close attention to her likes and habits that he could predict which plant she'd stop at, which flower would catch her attention. And there, hidden among the petals of a rose, she'd find the small, rolled up paper with the words *Leirum U Oye Voli* written delicately on it.

I love you, Muriel. He had never said those words aloud, but then again, he never had to. They had been written a thousand times.

It was as she came to another turn in the path that she thought she heard something. Looking back, Muriel found no one there; just roses and a few small puff birds landing to scrounge around for food. She smiled at their presence, but as her eyes drew up and she faced the pathway again, she found she was entirely alone. No monks; no Callan.

Her throat tightened as the loneliness pushed against her as a breeze came through, fluttering her cloak and gown. She had hoped that maybe Callan would have found her, would have predicted she'd come here and make his return. It had been a small yearning, but one that caused her to stay in the garden longer than she had planned.

Making her way around another bend, Muriel found that the pathway split. Deciding to buy herself some more time, she chose the one that would take her deeper into the garden instead of back into the shadows of the cathedral. She kept her pace slow, allowing herself to imagine Callan with her, what he'd do to Davien when she told him of all the threats. Or, better yet, Davien's look once Callan was home, taking his rightful place.

There was another rustling of branches, and still finding no one, she assumed it was the birds again. The loneliness pressed in, and to combat it, she pulled out the small cloth from her bodice and unfolded it, reading those familiar words again. "You're alive," she breathed out, allowing the words to warm her. But the question came without warning, a sad reminder that the nightmare wasn't over, that Davien might still somehow win. "But where are you?"

She rubbed her fingers against the cloth, knowing he had touched it once; that it was probably his own blood he had used. This was the closest she had been to him in nearly five years.

Another small rustling of branches erupted, but this time Muriel didn't bother to check. All she was focused on was the cloth and those words, her determination to find him igniting like a flame.

What she didn't see was the man standing far behind her, hidden amongst the roses at the bend in the path.

She also didn't see the pistol aimed right at her.

CHAPTER THIRTEEN

If keeping up with Callan was hard before, it was damn near impossible now.

Joss jogged just to match his strides, and there were moments when it wasn't him she was keeping her sights on. Henik remained ahead of her, his familiar form being the middle ground between prince and executioner. Normally, Joss wouldn't have had so much trouble, but the ax underneath her arm and the revolver against her side made moving at that pace a little awkward.

Brushing past pedestrians and carts, Callan came to a sudden stop again, allowing Joss and Henrik to reach him. It wasn't for their benefit, however; he had stopped because the two figures he had been chasing were walking up the steps of the cathedral. Guards were coming and going, the reason Callan was hesitating. But despite the pause, Joss could see that Callan's attention, while still aware of his surroundings, was focused primarily on Muriel.

Joss looked at the massive structure, admiring the towers, the arches, the stained-glass windows. Her mouth dropped open at the sight of it, which she quickly shut when Callan suddenly moved, crossing the street. Despite following him, Henrik looked back at Joss, worried.

She looked at him in understanding. They had never been to a church before, had never been allowed because of Joss's executioner bloodline. They didn't know the etiquette or rules, nor did they know if the same rules applied to them as they did back at home. But Callan was too important to lose, and so both chased after him. Keeping their heads low behind their hoods, they jogged up the steps to the cathedral doors that Callan had discreetly opened, peering in.

"Stay behind me," he murmured over his shoulder before slinking inside.

Joss hesitated, years of being denied rushing at her. It felt traitorous going in, knowing she wasn't welcomed. She detected that Henrik felt the same way when he looked at her again for reassurance. With a nod, they both slipped in, the door closing quietly behind them.

It took a second for the two to become adjusted to the view. The inside was just as massive as the outside, giant buttresses hung overhead as the stained-glass patterns cast their colors across the aisleway. The entire place held an echo of silence, a hushed presence of something otherworldly. A few people were scattered about, but no one had turned around. Seeing the citizens made both Joss and Henrik feel like intruders, knowing they were breaking a hidden law.

Her heart beat in her ears as she took in the scene, seeing Muriel and the man reaching a crossroads in the aisle before turning left. Off to the right, hidden among the shadows against the wall, was Callan's hooded form stalking after them.

Nudging Henrik, who was still gawking at the sight, the two made their way to Callan, trying to be as quiet as possible. He moved to one of the large pillars where the other aisle began, hiding in the shadows of the side aisle while peering from behind the solid stone. His eyes were locked on the couple.

Coming to stand with him, Joss peeked around Callan to find Muriel across the way on the other side of the aisleway, her companion still with her.

Looking up at Callan, she found his jaw was set underneath his hood, his stare hardening into something predatory.

"That's Davien with her, isn't it?" Joss whispered, and only a curt nod from him told her she was right.

Joss pulled back from the scene, standing in front of Henrik who was keeping his back on the pillar next to Callan, clearly uncomfortable being there. He was looking around, still taking it all in, when his gaze fell on Joss.

"You okay?" she mouthed to him, to which he grimaced a little.

Moving closer, he whispered in her ear, "I feel like we shouldn't be here."

"This isn't Galmoor," Joss reassured him. "No one knows who we are."

The worry remained, but the words seemed to break the tension as he took an easier breath.

Callan, however, hadn't moved.

Curious to see more, Joss moved to the other side of Henrik, staying hidden in the shadows while peeking out from the other side of the pillar. She found that no one in the pews had lifted their heads, each person lost deeply in their thoughts and prayers.

Able to see Muriel, she watched as the princess stood in front of rows of tiny candles, lighting one of them. The small dots of candlelight and the stained-glass window of the rose made the scene more mystical, enveloping the area in a warmth of pink and red light that made Joss stare in wonderment. A small part of her was almost envious of it, feeling an ache for the romantic scene that wasn't for her. And while the emotion gnawed at her, she smiled for Callan, knowing what he had been through and that this was what he deserved. *This*, she thought. *This is exactly where they were meant to reunite.*

It was as she stared that something moved out of the corner of her eye, catching her attention. Someone entered the cathedral behind them. By how they walked, it was a man, though the hood and cloak concealed his identity well. Instead of turning right like they had, the figure went left, stopping behind a far pillar that hid him from sight, making him oblivious to Muriel and Davien who were just down the aisleway.

An unsettling feeling came over her, and Joss moved around Henrik, coming to stand next to Callan again. "Callan," she was whispering right when his body tightened, and he lunged forward.

It was muscle memory in the way her hand grabbed his arm and her body turned, pinning him in place against the pillar. Joss had been around prisoners for so long, helping to wrangle them in place during interrogations, trials, and executions, that she didn't have to think; her body knew exactly how to respond.

Henrik also reacted, his good hand clamped down on the area between Callan's neck and shoulder as if holding him back. Both knew where the pulse was, and with the right amount of pressure applied, it would cause fainting or at least some lightheadedness they could use in their favor. It was a method they had used a few times, a last-ditch effort to stop whoever they were trying to contain. However, by how Henrik stared back at her, Joss understood the cloak would make it harder for him to apply pressure. If the man of war really wanted to get away, there was nothing stopping him. Henrik was too used to helping her though, so it was all he could do to assist.

A snarl escaped Callan as both tried holding him back, and Joss hoped the sound hadn't echoed. She glanced across the way at Muriel, seeing that Davien had her by the wrist, unaware of who was watching. It wasn't hard to see that he was threatening her by how her body had tensed.

"Let me go," Callan growled as he tried to shove them away, his gaze darkening.

"We're not alone," Joss hissed back.

Callan was about to yank himself free when the words hit him and he stopped, peering around the pillar and following Joss's gaze to the figure in the far corner. He blinked, processing the threat. Sinking back against the pillar, Callan held himself back, Joss keeping her hand on his arm in case he decided otherwise. It wasn't until he placed his hand on hers, much more gently than anticipated, that she finally let him go. Joss glanced over at Henrik, finding he too had released him.

The revolver in her waistband had come loose in their

scuffle, which Joss quickly fixed as she kept her attention on Muriel. She watched as the princess pulled violently away from Davien and fled out a side door. Callan shifted his stance, teeth bared as Davien took a few steps after her but stopped. He stood for a moment until finally turning away, marching down the side aisle to the hooded figure at the end. Their exchange was brief, just long enough to prove they knew each other, and then both men left.

The cathedral door barely closed when Callan shot forward, his steps quick as he went after Muriel. Joss and Henrik kept up, side-eyeing those sitting in the pews and thankful they were all still preoccupied.

Escaping out of the alcove, the three were met with the blaring sunlight. Following an alley-like path, the cathedral wall remained on one side while a tall stone wall lined with thick rose bushes stood guard on the other. Joss shifted her ax a little from underneath her arm, trying to keep a good hold on the weapon as she trailed after Callan, Henrik right behind her.

Callan stopped at the corner of the cathedral, the garden stretching out before him. Joss felt the heat of the sun on her as she took in the deep smells of roses. The garden was beautiful, the roses in all shades of color she hadn't seen before. Off to the side was a separate building attached to the cathedral, a miniature in size but equally splendid.

"Wow," Henrik breathed out next to her, taken aback by the sight.

"We used to meet here," Callan murmured, nodding to the garden. "And that's the chapter house," he pointed out.

A couple of hooded figures were walking towards it, buckets

in their hands. "Monks," Callan assessed before looking over the garden again.

Finding no one else, he proceeded forward to the closest pathway, disappearing into the garden.

"Should we follow?" Henrik asked.

Joss felt the same, wanting to give Callan and his wife privacy yet not trusting their surroundings. "Just in case," she replied, following Callan into the garden.

The rose bushes were thicker than she realized, creating fragranced walls that formed mazes. Rounding a bend, she found Callan making his way around another bend, following the trails by memory. While she would have loved to have lingered, enjoying the walk, the threat of past attacks crept up on her, and both she and Henrik quietly hurried to reach him. A breeze rustled through as they found him, standing where two pathways split. He was listening, they realized. Looking over his shoulder to make sure it was them approaching, Joss found that the hardness earlier had disappeared, replaced by something more—hope, longing.

Deciding on a path, Callan continued on, Joss and Henrik following along. It wasn't until they reached another bend that Callan suddenly stopped, his eyes widening, his face flooded with emotions.

He found her. She couldn't keep the smile from showing, slowing down a distance away to give Callan some privacy. Henrik, too, slowed down, coming to stand behind her.

"You're alive."

The voice came out as a soft murmur, filtering in from the other side of the rose bushes. Joss held her breath, realizing Muriel was across from them, hidden behind the foliage. The words were a statement, as if she were talking to herself.

"But where are you?" The princess was asking no one in particular.

Joss looked at Callan as if answering her question. Muriel's tone matched the longing in Callan's eyes. He had just pulled his hood off, taking a step forward when something in the bush next to him rustled a bit, causing the prince to halt. Cold shock flooded his face before darkening into a shade of anger. But he didn't move, didn't say anything. His eyes moved from the bush to Muriel, and then to Joss, who stared back in anticipation.

Something was wrong.

Turning around to Henrik, Joss felt the gasp catch in her throat. A pistol was pushed up against Henrik's temple, a hooded figure standing right behind him, the grey mask staring at her from behind Henrik's shoulder. It was just like back in Raspshire, right before the arrow struck Henrik's previous attacker.

This time, however, there was no arrow. The figure remained behind him, staring back at Joss before raising a finger to where his lips would be, telling her to keep quiet, and then pointed forward, directing her to go to Callan.

Seeing the panic in Henrik's face, the way he swallowed hard to keep his anxiety down, she reached her hand out to him, which he caught, his gloved hand tightly holding hers. Never turning around, Joss walked backwards, making sure to keep her eyes on Henrik, letting him know he wasn't alone, that they were in this together.

The two quietly moved to Callan, halting only when the rose

bushes prevented them from moving forward. With Henrik and his attacker in front of her, Joss peered over at Callan, whose back was now on the other side of her. That's when she caught sight of the end of a rifle protruding from the rose bush, pressing so hard against his neck that it was leaving an indent. Joss's stomach turned, knowing that if she did pull out the revolver against her waistband, the two men on either side of her would be dead.

Another masked figure was coming down the pathway, their footsteps surprisingly quiet against the dirt. They stopped about where Henrik and Joss had been standing, and raised a pistol into the rose bush, quietly stepping forward, the gun disappearing quietly into the foliage.

They were taking aim at Muriel.

Callan shifted, his muscles trembling, wanting to fight. "Easy," someone whispered, so softly it could have been mistaken for the breeze blowing by.

"Your Highness!"

Everyone flinched at the sound, a woman's voice yelling in the distance.

There was a faint rustling of fabric, and Joss assumed Muriel was hurrying to the voice. "I'm here!" she called back, her voice farther away.

Callan's body teetered, his hand slightly twitching, wanting to reach out for her to come back but being unable to.

"Your Highness, my apologies, but you're needed in the king's chambers," the other woman was saying, her words obscured by both distance and the denseness of the rose bushes.

Everyone stood still, waiting for more, but nothing came.

Muriel left, leaving behind the threat she hadn't known was there, nor the husband that had come back for her.

Henrik's hand squeezed hers, and looking up into his face, she saw the worry in his hazel eyes. "What's happening?" he mouthed, needing to focus on anything else but the cold steel pressed against his skin.

A couple more masked figures were coming up behind when Joss mouthed back, "We lost."

CHAPTER FOURTEEN

Consumed by darkness, Aric pressed his hands against the wooden walls and proceeded down the stairwell at a snail's pace. Twice, he almost misjudged a step, and while he regained himself quickly and learned what pace he needed to not make the same mistake twice, he still kicked himself for being stuck in such a situation.

With the knife in hand, he proceeded on, wondering if he was going to run into anyone. The muffled music of the parlors seeped in from behind the walls, and as he followed the spiral path, the music rose as he continued downward until nothing was left to hear except his own heart rate.

It was only a few short seconds after the music faded into nothing that he heard the distant sound of voices. The darkness didn't help, trapping him in an abyss led him right to it. Keeping his gait steady and quiet, he crept on until finally he took a step and realized he met the ground. Blinking, he saw a faint light ahead, showing a turn in the corridor.

Holding his breath, he inched along the wall, gripping the knife tighter as the voices became clearer. Taking in the damp smells and the way the walls felt under his touch—packed in dirt with a few oddly placed beams and stones to hold areas in place—he knew exactly where he was.

Traitor's Alley.

He used these tunnels sparingly, only for quick escapes when need be. Being down underneath the city had never been his choice of scenery, the tunnels being the physical underbelly of Aselian. In fact, for most criminals, the tunnels were frequented as little as possible, despite how beneficial they could be. There were just too many legends, too many horror stories giving the tunnels their eeriness, and even Aric wasn't always immune to the way a tale rattled his nerves.

Creeping onward, he came to the turn, his hooded form peering carefully around the corner.

The electrical lights overhead provided ample light to see by, revealing two cloaked individuals in a small room, one standing up while another was bent down in the corner, his back to Aric. Fixing his gaze on it, Aric could make out a wrapped-up body in front of the hunched-over figure. He only knew because he had wrapped bodies like that before, mainly to move them to a different location so nature could help conceal his attack, either by water or some wild animal needing a good meal. It all depended on how "natural" the paying customer wanted the death to look.

"I don't know why he doesn't just kill them," the one standing was saying, and while his hood concealed his identity, the muffled tone gave away that he was wearing a mask.

Aric's nerves jolted, gripping the knife handle harder as the memory of the beatings came back to him. He couldn't wait to repay them the favor when he got the chance.

"He wants to have his fun first," the hunched over one was saying, his voice much deeper and older than his companion.

He, Aric thought. They must be talking about the Mask, their leader. Obviously, these were only his minions doing his bidding.

Another figure emerged from the side, and Aric felt his pulse in his neck, a rush of adrenaline coming at the prospects of taking on all three men. If he had brought his crossbow, he would have evened the odds a little in his favor, given that hand-to-hand combat was going to be tricky in such a tight space.

"Here, take this to him," the hunched over man said, handing a small bundle to the third man. Taking it, the man left, disappearing down what Aric assumed was another tunnel.

"We can't use his own?" the standing mask was saying, his companion remaining hunched over.

"The harlot is still busy with him," the other replied, wrapping the body back up. "It'll take too long to retrieve, especially since he has them now."

He has them now...

Jocelyn, Aric thought. While Henrik and Callan also came to mind, it was the thought of Jocelyn that made his jaw clench. His heart skipped, eyes narrowing in a need to attack these men and get to her. The emotion swarmed him so intently he had to hold himself against the wall so he wouldn't proceed in killing them.

But then the first statement replayed in his mind, the comment about the harlot. They were talking about *him,* but what did he have that the Mask needed to retrieve so badly? Especially if he already had Jocelyn and the others.

Leverage. He could hear the Mask saying the word again. That conversation back in the cottage was like a bad dream he couldn't shake. *What the hell do I have that you'll use against them?* Aric growled in thought.

"What if she doesn't kill him?"

The hunched over man stood up, facing his companion. While his mask hid his expression, his body language gave him away. "Stop worrying. The wench thinks she's becoming queen after all this."

Shit, it is *one of the princes*, Aric bit back, remembering the look in Andrina's eyes when he commented that she had been paid handsomely for killing him. It was handsome; the prize had been the throne.

"She'll kill him," the man continued. "She already helped extract his contacts. They're either dead now or will turn against him in the same way. So even if Aric Kayden makes it out of that room, he'll have nowhere to go. He's dead no matter what."

A chuckle rumbled in the air, and then the two departed, disappearing out of the room. Aric could still hear them talking, mentioning Andrina's name and the phonograph. They spoke of vulgar things, making Aric a little glad he had killed his old friend. She died believing her life would change for the better, which seemed much more merciful than to let her learn that she was being used in more ways than one; just a means for another man's gain.

Aric stayed where he was, listening for any other movement. When none came, he rounded the turn and quietly approached the small room. In the far wall was one of the other tunnels, the string of lights flickering along the dugout corridor. Seeing no one else, Aric approached the wrapped body lying against the wall. Peeling back the end of the sheet, he came face-to-face with a man about his age, his skin ashen, revealing he'd only been dead a couple short hours. He also had blonde hair, about as long as Aric's and resting against his shoulders. Narrowing his eyes, Aric touched a section of the hair that seemed shorter, finding a chunk of the strands cut.

Pressing his lips together, he dropped the hair and flipped the sheet back over the body. Standing back up, he kept his eyes on the dead form. He only knew one reason someone would take locks of hair like that.

Proof of death.

He cursed under his breath, realizing the Mask had him. His contacts were gone, or at least turned against him, and now anyone the Mask sought would believe he was dead. It would be an easy lie, especially if Aric never showed up.

Closing his eyes, Aric breathed hard through his nose, the earthy aroma overwhelming him. *Don't believe him, Jocelyn,* he thought to her, holding the knife in a death grip, reminding himself that he was still very much alive. *I'm going to find you, as I promised.*

When he opened his eyes, Aric pulled away from the body, leveling his glare on the tunnel, his mind set on death. Because if he was already considered a dead man, then he might as well take as many of those assholes with him as possible.

You swear? Jocelyn's words whispered into his mind again, and as he made his way down the tunnel after the masked men, he repeated his answer.

On my life.

CHAPTER FIFTEEN

Muriel hurried down the corridor, her ladies-in-waiting trailing after her. The one who fetched her from the cathedral's garden was right behind.

"They've called all the physicians," she was saying again, increasingly out of breath as they went. "They've tried everything—"

Muriel turned the corner, the king's chamber doors wide open with a slew of guards standing around. Pages were being dispatched, one nearly running into Muriel since she hadn't moved out of his way fast enough.

And then came the scream.

Muriel came to an instant stop when she heard it. It was guttural, almost animal in the way it hung in the air, and Muriel covered her own mouth so she wouldn't join it.

The guards parted then, and there, almost emotionless, was Davien. Muriel watched the whole thing in slow motion: the way the guards kneeled, the way Davien stood a little straighter. His head turned like a snake, catching sight of her.

Tears blurred her vision as she watched Davien come towards her, a few of the guards standing up and following him, and she realized to her dismay that it was his own knights. The rest stood but remained where they were, as if they were in a daze.

"The council is being summoned," Davien was saying as he came to stand in front of her, taking over her entire vision.

Muriel slowly dropped her hand, searching Davien's face for anything: grief, resentment, anything human.

"You will come with me to deliver the news of the king's passing," he was explaining before snapping his fingers, a couple of his knights moving towards her ladies-in-waiting.

"What are you doing?" Muriel demanded, watching as the girls huddled closer behind her.

"You and your ladies must be in proper attire." He scanned her over, disapproving of her wardrobe. "The royal family must be present."

Muriel looked him over again, the screaming sobs relentlessly playing in the background. "May we not mourn him first?" she asked quietly, knowing Charisse couldn't be left alone. She needed family, someone to lean on.

"You can mourn for him the rest of your life, if you wish," Davien shrugged. "But the crown must be passed to the next heir immediately. Tradition says it."

Mors Exitus, Muriel thought. She knew the old law, had even thought of using it herself in case the time called for it. Due to its rules, as well as past conflicts and uprisings, the royal family always became nervous when a king died. The need to hand over the crown to the next heir as quickly as possible was imperative so there would be no break in the family line. The royal family, and those who benefited from them, wouldn't breathe easy until the crown was secure on the next king's head, who was one of their own.

This time, however, Davien was using the tradition to his benefit.

He's dead, Muriel's mind whispered. Tears sprang from her eyes, running down her cheeks as she glared back at the prince. "I must see him first," she said, moving past Davien and needing to see the king for herself.

On shaky legs, Muriel walked to the chamber doors, the guards who were lingering around bowing to her. Coming to the doorway, she came to a slow stop. The physicians were pulling Charisse from the bed, holding her as she tried to claw her way back to her husband. The king himself was still, and as Muriel drew closer, she watched his chest where his ashen hands were folded. There was no rising of his breath, no signs of any movement.

"Your Majesty," she said out loud, as if he was listening to her. "It's been confirmed that your son, Callan Ronen, is alive."

A hush fell in the room, and even Charisse's sobs fell back into whimpers.

"How dare you," a growl came from behind, and Muriel didn't have to turn around to know it was Davien.

"He's home," Muriel continued, a small smile on her face, imagining the king's eyes opening, the look of relief that would have crossed his face. "He made it home, Your Majesty. And I know he made it home," she said, turning around to find Davien just a couple steps behind her, "because I heard *you* confirm it."

Davien's eyes widened in a rage she had never seen before. "I confirmed nothing," he said quietly, straining.

"I heard you," Muriel said pointedly, another tear falling despite her confident gaze.

"You heard nothing," Davien snarled, taking a step forward.

"Threaten me all you want. You've done it for years." Muriel matched his snarl, her now blood-shot eyes glaring at him. "But my husband is alive and he's here and he will take the crown. So whatever moment you think you're about to have, you better relish in it, because it will not last long."

Davien stared at her, and at first Muriel was surprised he wasn't responding. But then suddenly his face changed, his arm swung, and she was struck hard on the side of the face. His hit sent her sideways, but she staggered, catching herself before falling. Backing away from him, she hit the end of the bed, cradling her stinging face, blood flooding from her nostrils and dripping over her lips. She could taste it as she breathed hard, her body trembling as she stared at him.

"Clean her up," he ordered, and as he marched out of the room, Muriel realized that his men had already entered, her ladies-in-waiting outside looking in with horrified faces.

Just as two of the knights came forward to escort her, Muriel looked to the physicians, each one looking away as if they hadn't seen anything. Because if anyone ever asked if the Prince Royal had struck her, they could all deny it.

Cowards, she glared, until she found one person staring right at her.

Charisse stared back with tear-soaked eyes, her appearance

disheveled for the first time in her life. But what looked like shock quickly turned into disappointment until she gasped, grief reminding her of what she had lost. After taking a couple deep breaths, she regained her footing from the physicians, who quietly let her go. She stood a little taller, much like her son just moments ago in the hallway.

Muriel watched in dismay as the queen pressed a hand to her chest, let out another shaking sob before she put it all away—the crying, the screams, the emotions. While tears still tried to trail down her cheeks, Charisse ignored them, her stoic demeanor coming back to her. With an authoritative tone Muriel had never heard before, Charisse said pointedly, "Follow your king."

Muriel didn't feel the hand on her arm as she was led out of the chambers, the blood from her nose now dripping down her dress. The cold fear crawled under her skin, terrorizing her into thinking that Callan wouldn't make it in time, that Davien would follow through with his threats, and that the hope she had clung to all those years was now dead, along with their king.

CHAPTER SIXTEEN

The chapter house was nothing in size compared to the cathedral, and yet Joss was enamored by it. Or at least she would have been if the gun weren't pointed at her.

While the masked figure removed the gun from Henrik's temple, he now walked behind them, aiming at both. The three were stripped of their weapons, causing Joss to feel empty without her ax—and the revolver, for that matter—which was being carried by a masked figure who trailed behind them all.

Joss and Henrik were led behind Callan, who had the luxury of two masked goons escorting him, pistols aimed at his head. Obviously, they knew of his warrior reputation, taking no chance in leaving him alone with one guard. While his hands remained raised, Joss noted the tension in his shoulders, the way he strolled through the chapter house doors as if he owned the place. In retrospect, he did, but it was obvious it was more to show power against the men who held him captive, a future king to the very end.

Entering the building, Joss took in the ornate room with the beautiful wood chairs, the stained-glass windows splashing colors across the stone walls. In between the windows were bookshelves lined with all kinds of thick, leather-bound books. In any other circumstance, Joss would have loved to search through the collection. She didn't know what kind of books they were, but given the gold lettering on the spines, they seemed old but important, ancient wisdom surrounding the meeting hall for the monks.

In the middle of the room, surrounded by a circle of chairs, they noticed a solid slab of stone with a crest of a rose on it. Brought to a stop in front of it, Joss noticed the rose was remarkably similar to the one in the stained glass.

There was a moment of silence, and looking over, Joss found one of the masked men walking over to a cast iron sconce, one of many lining the room. Each one was empty, the electrical lights above taking the place of the torch light that once was used. Pulling on it, the sconce shifted away from the wall like a lever. A crack in the floor echoed into the room, and to her amazement, the stone with the rose crest slid down before shifting to the side, revealing a hidden staircase.

Looking at Henrik, she found him equally baffled. Callan, however, continued to look angry, unmoved by the display.

Masked men pushing them forward, they were led down the spiraling stairs, coming into a room that was much smaller than the one above them. Lights were strung around the walls, enveloping the area in a dimness that made the impacted dirt walls look more stone-like. The dampen earth smell was overwhelming as they came to the end of the stairs, facing another hooded figure who was waiting for them.

"This way," he instructed, and the three were moved along with him, following him into the arched tunnel. The string of lights followed them down, flickering occasionally and making Joss a little nervous, wondering if they were about to go out. When the tunnel turned, coming to a crossroads, Callan seemed confused.

Glancing over his shoulder at them, Joss noticed that something was wrong. "This is new," he commented, only facing forward when one of the gunmen pushed him along to keep following.

Joss and Henrik stayed quiet as the newly developed tunnel threw them out into another room, bigger than the last. There, sitting in a chair with a masked figure standing on either side, was yet another masked individual, this one chuckling to himself.

"Ah, if it isn't His Royal Highness." The man seemed to smile behind his mask, rising as Callan, Joss, and Henrik were brought to stand before him. "You, sir, have been a very hard man to catch."

"I'm a very hard man to keep as well," Callan replied, trying to scoff off the comment, though the edge in his voice revealed his anger.

"Your wit knows no bounds," the masked man chuckled as one of the other figures moved the chair to the corner of the room. The three watched as the men deposited their weapons on the chair, out of reach.

"So, who are you?" Callan demanded, not wanting to play into the man's games.

"I usually go by as the Mask, like I told one of your friends," the man remarked. "But you of all people should know who I really am."

The Mask. Joss's breath quickened, remembering Aric telling her about him. This was the man who had been after them, who beat Aric, the whole reason they met. She still remembered the way they found him, bruised and bleeding, wondering who could have inflicted so much damage on a person.

Glancing at Callan, she found to her dismay that he was staring at the man in confusion. He was more taken aback than all of them, which meant only one thing.

This wasn't Davien.

"Oh, come now," the Mask chided, standing in front of Callan. "Don't tell me that you don't remember me."

Callan searched the man's eyes and around the mask, trying to find any hints of resemblance. The mask's eye sockets were narrower than most, making it hard to distinguish any skin color that might have peeked through.

"Disappointing," the Mask confirmed, "but not surprising. You never were one to give me the time of day."

The Mask moved on, coming to stand in front of both Joss and Henrik. "You two, however, are extremely surprising. An executioner by day, a healer by night," he commented, looking right at Joss. "I admit, in your position, healing would be the last thing I'd be doing. And you—" he turned to Henrik "—I'm surprised you stayed in such conditions. As a street urchin once, you of all people could have left and survived." He looked back at Joss. "Just like your brother, who seems to be doing quite well for himself."

While her nerves twitched, Joss stood her ground. He knew all about them, even Oliver.

"So, what do you want?" Callan growled. "Or is your plan to

talk us to death?"

The Mask genuinely laughed, remaining in front of Joss. "Oh, little prince, that temper of yours—" he shook his head "—is just like your father's. Always so impatient."

"You haven't seen what my impatience can do," Callan growled again, ignoring the Mask's flippant comment.

Amused, the Mask moved slowly towards him, coming to stand in front of him again. "How about I show you mine instead?"

There was no warning when Henrik was suddenly yanked to the side, being dragged by two figures. Joss lunged for him but was caught around the waist. Something tripped her, and she was thrown sideways to the ground, her shoulder hitting the hard dirt. Suddenly, her arms were grabbed, and while she tried to fight them, her hands were nonetheless tied behind her back. Searching for Henrik, she found him near the far wall, face first to the ground while his own wrists were tied behind his back.

Callan, however, remained standing, and when Joss looked up at him, she found a masked figure with the end of his pistol aimed right at his face.

"Your fight is with *me*!" Callan was still demanding, despite the threat. "Let them go!"

"Or what?" the Mask chuckled, rising to his feet after finishing with Joss's wrists. "Do they mean something to you?"

Callan didn't reply, but Joss was too concerned with Henrik to pay attention to him. It wasn't until someone kicked the lad in the stomach that she found her own voice. "Leave him alone! He hasn't done anything to you!"

A boot obstructed her vision, and turning her head up, she

found the Mask squatting down in front of her, shielding her from Henrik's view. "Oh, but he has. Both of you have."

Joss searched for Callan, finding that he was being moved off to the side. The gun once pointed at him was replaced by two masked men who held him back as a third was binding his hands behind him.

"You two," the Mask continued, gaining back her attention, "were supposed to kill *him*, and you failed. And now, he's here." He pointed in Callan's direction, which Joss didn't bother following now that she knew where he was.

"This lesson is for you, deathsman." The Mask stood up then, moving slowly away.

Joss was met with the curled version of Henrik, his head bowed, his sides heaving from the pain of being hit. Before she had a chance to call out to him, the Mask's voice interrupted.

"I'll give you one chance, Your Highness. I'll let you go, I'll let your friends here go, I'll make sure your wife meets you unharmed. All you have to do is leave. Throw down your birthright and never return."

Joss turned her head again, eyeing Callan. What she noticed wasn't just silence; it was a subtle rebellion. He answered without having to say anything.

"Exactly," the Mask answered. "You would sacrifice those who care about you for the crown."

Callan opened his mouth but then shut it.

Joss heard the crunching of boots against the dirt as her vision was blocked again, and the Mask knelt in front of her. "That is the kind of man you saved," he whispered.

"What did you expect?" she asked, her voice raw as she lay there.

The Mask tilted his head, curious.

"You're asking an heir to the throne to turn away from a lifetime of conditioning," Joss continued. "So of course that's his answer. He doesn't know any other way."

"And that doesn't bother you?" the Mask mused.

"I'm an executioner," she reminded him. "I also have been conditioned not to feel in certain circumstances."

"You sure?" the Mask asked, and something in the way he said it made Joss hesitate. "Everyone has a breaking point," he continued, "even that assassin. I can see why you like him, though. Golden hair, green eyes—there's a lot of competition for him, you know."

Joss felt the heat in her cheeks. She hadn't lied to herself that there was someone better for Aric, but just mentioning him in that way made her blush, something she wasn't used to. His looks, his persona—the asshole in front of her wasn't wrong.

Green eyes. Her mind suddenly coiled around the words, something not sitting right with her. Aric's eyes weren't both green.

Her breath caught then. If this were the Mask, the man who had tortured Aric, he would have known that. He would have known Aric's eyes were different, one green and one grey, which meant...

"I'm curious, prince," the Mask was saying, his attention fixed on Callan.

Fully bound, Callan stood his ground.

"What exactly was your plan in coming back?"

Joss held her breath, looking at Henrik. He had lifted his head up, resting his cheek against the dirt. As he stared back at her, confusion twisted itself into his expression.

For a man who had hired an assassin to kill them, the Mask was sure taking his time in killing them now.

He's stalling. The thought woke her up, causing her to turn her head to see Callan. He glanced at her, and just as she was about to tell him, she found one of the masked men next to him eyeing her, causing her to stay silent.

"It doesn't really matter now, does it?" Callan grumbled.

"Indulge me," the Mask seemed to smile.

Joss's stomach fluttered with anxiousness, needing Callan to know they weren't dealing with the right man, when something vibrated into the air. There was an echo, loud and deep, that the underground muffled. Looking back at Henrik, she saw that he too had heard it.

The room suddenly went silent, everyone else listening in, noticing the faint sound. It wasn't until the echo developed a rhythm that Joss knew what it was.

The cathedral bell.

A shadow filtered through the tunnel, a figure running towards them as a scuffle started behind, Callan bolting forward while the Mask's henchmen held him back, eventually pushing him against the wall. He tried fighting them, even with his hands behind his back, which ended with a grunt as they pushed him down to the ground like they had with Joss and Henrik.

The figure emerged into the room, heading straight to the Mask. Soft words were exchanged, a hesitation, and then the Mask followed the messenger out of the room. Callan screamed into the dirt behind her, and Joss craned her neck to see him, finding bodies shuffling around him, his captors holding him down.

Henrik watched the scene wide-eyed as Joss allowed her head to rest against the dirt, her heart breaking for Callan.

Although soft, the exchange of words was loud enough for everyone to hear.

The king was dead.

CHAPTER SEVENTEEN

The vibrations of the bell eventually ceased, and Joss continued to lay there, listening to Callan. He had been breathing hard, his adrenaline up, but that had quieted. Henrik also remained placid, watching the masked figures come and go. The news of the king's death had sent them into a frenzy, another unknown plan unfolding around them.

It wasn't until another left, the last one hovering in the entrance way with his back to them that she heard the squeaking of rope. Turning her head, she caught sight of Callan's shoulder jerk as he tried to free his wrists. Even in his misery, he was in survival mode.

The guard heard it too, turning his gaze onto the prince. Stalking forward, the masked figure was just rounding past Joss when she kicked the man in the ankle and caused him to stumble.

No words were exchanged as the figure regained himself, strode over, and threw his boot into her back in one swift kick. The air escaped her lungs as pain seized her body, grazing the area that Master Greyson bruised when they had fought. She slowly rolled onto her stomach, the ground comforting her as her back throbbed from the strike.

Henrik was yelling her name, but she couldn't focus on anything else except the pain. Squeezing her eyes shut and seething in the dirt didn't help much, either. Her stomach knotted, still sensitive ever since the poisoning. Joss almost thought she'd hurl right there, and it took everything in her to keep breathing as the pain ever so slowly began to recede.

Opening her eyes, she found Callan breathing heavily as well, tears streaming down his cheeks which didn't match the furious look on his face. He knew the king was dead by the fact that the cathedral bell rang, but the exchange between the messenger and the Mask confirmed it.

Finding Callan still tied, the boot steps rounded past her, going back to check on the tunnel. Joss found Callan watching the left-behind guard before his gaze met hers.

"He's not the Mask," she mouthed out, shaking her head as her heavy breaths caused the dirt in front of her to move.

His eyebrows furrowing was the only sign he had heard her. He moved his body sideways, laying against his shoulder as his other arm jerked behind him as he worked. Years of being a prisoner of war suddenly became useful in those few minutes.

Suddenly, he stopped, his gaze hardening as he stared at something behind her.

Joss was about to rotate around when something heavy pressed hard against her back, pinning her to the ground. The weight made her chest feel like it was going to be crushed, the air coming in and out in gasps as her chin scraped the floor. Her neck ached as she turned her head, finding someone standing over her. Then the weight dug in, proving it was a boot.

"Let me have a moment with them," the Mask's voice spoke up overhead, causing the second pair of footsteps to fade into the distance, the guard who had kicked her now leaving.

"Get off of her!" Henrik screamed, which was easily ignored by the Mask's laughter.

The boot heel dug in deeper, as if making a point. The gasps became auditory, a whine escaping as her chest felt constricted.

"Look at the company you've kept," the Mask called out to Callan, who simply glared at him as he came to a sitting position. "Death follows you everywhere. First, it was your mother, and I'm assuming a slew of friends and colleagues followed during that war you were in. And now, your father. Maybe it's you." There was a deep chuckle, amusement in those words. "It's ironic you'd become acquaintances with a deathsman and her assistant. They know death, so no wonder they were the only ones to give you the time of day. And here you sit, Your Highness, ready to give them up easily if you had to."

Joss's vision blurred as she seethed through her teeth, trying to fight through the pain. It wasn't until the boot was forcibly removed, the pressure lifted, that her lungs involuntarily gasped as air rushed into her. She heard the Mask stumble into the wall, and through her tear-stained gaze she caught sight of the Mask regaining himself.

"You stupid boy," he growled, and Joss could hear footsteps scuffing against the dirt behind her, rolling her body to the side in time to see Henrik backing away. He had gotten himself up, shoving the Mask off her, and now didn't know what to do since his hands were still bound. The determination was still there, but so was the fear.

"I guess you'll have to be the next lesson," the Mask determined, his boots crunching in the dirt as he stepped over Joss, making her shudder, the phantom of his boot still in between her shoulder blades.

"Henrik!" she called out, the Mask obstructing her view of him.

Suddenly, something dark rushed at the Mask from behind, and it took a second for Joss to realize it was Callan, his one hand freed. He grabbed the Mask around the neck, putting him into a headlock. Dragging him backwards, Joss rolled farther out of the way, dodging a kick from the Mask who was flailing, unable to get a handle on either Callan or the ground. As he was about to get a good standing, Henrik darted to him, kicking him in the shin and causing him to collapse right into Callan's death grip.

There were gurgles, seething, and even the mask itself had shifted, causing the man to look faceless.

"Get me your dagger!" Callan exclaimed through bared teeth.

With his arms still tied, Henrik staggered to the chair, bending over awkwardly to get ahold of the blade handle.

Joss, despite the pain in her back, carefully came to a sitting position and then rose to her feet, stepping forward to face the Mask. Seeing that Henrik didn't need any help, she placed herself in front of the next threat, knowing another good kick would keep the Mask in his place.

How Callan was handling him, it was obvious he didn't need her help. Callan was like a statue, holding the struggling man by the neck. The sounds the man made were ugly, but what was louder was the silence that came as the Mask's arms finally fell against his sides, the life squeezed out of him.

"Your dagger," Callan called out, and Henrik came to his side, turning around so Callan could grab the dagger from his bound hands.

In one fluid motion, the prince sank the blade deep into the base of the man's neck. If the strangling didn't kill him, the blade had.

"Just in case," he mumbled, allowing the body to drop to the ground. He proceeded to cut Henrik's bindings and, once the lad was free, motioned for Joss to turn around. He had cut the rope free of her wrists when his hand gently squeezed her arm.

"Are you alright?" he asked softly.

Joss stared into his dark eyes, realizing she was seeing his humanity, the part of him he guarded from everyone. It would be fleeting, she already knew, so she nodded, whispering a "yes." Callan then looked to Henrik with the same question, who gave the same response.

Nodding back, Callan's hardened gaze returned when he looked at the body, making his way towards it.

Joss rubbed her wrists as she watched over Callan, also curious to know who this man really was. Henrik had gone to the corner to gather their weapons, the lad clearly ready to leave.

Rolling the body over, Callan pulled the mask off, his body tensing.

"You know him?" Joss asked quietly.

"He grew up alongside Davien and Eiden, one of their friends when they were kids," Callan admitted. "They used to practice fighting in the gardens. He went off to training a year after Davien."

"So, what's wrong?" Joss asked, noticing that what the man had said caused more questions.

"I know it's been years, but... it didn't sound like him," Callan admitted, coming to stand on his feet. "He never used to talk like that. Even the way he spoke was... different."

"He was impersonating, I think because he was stalling."

Callan looked at her, his expression falling into a quiet realization. If the Mask was Davien, he wouldn't have been down there with them. He would have been by the king's bedside.

Callan swallowed hard, turning away from the scene. Henrik approached, and Callan took Joss's small pistol, placing it back in his boot. He then grabbed the revolver, leaving Henrik with his knife, which the lad put back inside his own boot. "We have to get to the castle. They'll announce the new king immediately, per tradition," he said as he worked.

Joss faced him as she stood between him and the tunnel, Henrik handing her the ax. Callan, however, refused to look at her, paying attention to the number of bullets in the cylinder.

"I'm so sorry," she whispered.

The prince bit his lip as he held the revolver tightly, his eyes immediately going to the ceiling. "We'll take the tunnel, which leads to a courtyard thankfully not too far from the Great Hall. That's where they normally announce such things."

He stared for a moment until finally he brought his gaze down. The pain became embedded in the lines in his face, and in the way his eyes were trying not to mist over. Joss knew that kind of pain. It was the kind of grief that changed people.

"The crown is what matters now," he said, his tone low, his voice hard, only because he was trying to keep himself composed. "We have to save it."

"Okay," she replied quietly, understanding. He had been denied coming home all those years, denied seeing his father when he was still alive. He couldn't save his father, but he could save the crown. The crown was the part of his father he still had.

Callan rounded past her, but before entering the tunnel, he stopped. Looking over his shoulder at them, he said, "You don't have to come with me. I'll find you both afterwards. I'll make this all right, like I said."

"We've already come this far." Joss shrugged, looking to Henrik who came to stand by her, also agreeing.

A small smile of gratitude revealed itself. "I wouldn't give either of you up," the prince admitted. "Not after everything you've gone through for me."

The dead man's words had bothered him. She assumed it had all been to aggravate them, and in some small way it had worked.

"We know," Henrik answered this time, Joss being the one to silently agree.

With an understanding laid out between them, Callan journeyed into the tunnel, Joss and Henrik following behind.

The dirt smelled rich as the tunnel enveloped them, the stringed light overhead illuminating the path in clear brightness, giving both Joss and Henrik a false kind of security. But upon reaching the original tunnels, they learned quickly why most would choose not to be down there.

While the string lights were fitted to allow enough ample lighting, they were clearly old, some of the bulbs long burnt out and making parts of the tunnel dim. Some flickered, threatening to give out as darkness edged into the tunnel any way it could. Spaced out were small sconces, waxed candles melted into the metal, formed into dripping sculptures that hardened with time. The air itself smelled of old earth and musk and something else—like death but older.

While Joss stayed in between Callan and Henrik, she still caught herself looking over her shoulder, making sure Henrik was still behind her and that no one had crept up on them.

"It's actually not too bad down here," Henrik admitted, trying to lighten the mood. "Are you sure no one uses it?"

"Some probably do, but not many," Callan replied, and as if answering him, a thudding sound came from inside the walls. All three came to a sudden halt, startled by it.

"Maybe it's... a gopher," Henrik suggested, causing the other two to look from the wall to him, eyebrows raised. "What? They can do a lot of damage," he defended when they continued on, not wanting an explanation.

However, it wasn't long before Callan came to a quiet stop again, the entrance to another tunnel revealing itself just in front of him. Peering around the corner, Callan kept the revolver in hand as he moved forward. Joss also checked, finding the string lights flickering along the ceiling as the tunnel curved to the right. As she was passing, something echoed like a muffled scream.

Joss stopped, ax in hand as she listened. Henrik came to stand next to her, both watching as the shadows hovered in the distance.

"It's probably no one," Callan said, keeping his voice down as he waited a few feet away.

"Then what is it?" Joss whispered.

Callan's lips turned into a grim line before he finally replied a little more normally, "Let's just say there's a reason why many don't come down here."

Another knock came from behind the wall, causing both to spin around and look.

Callan, not bothering to stay, continued, and Joss and Henrik quickly followed, not wanting to be left behind.

"When these tunnels were being built," Callan started to explain as their path turned, following it around, "they weren't by professionals. The copper mines weren't founded yet, and everyone here were just farmers or traders. A lot of people died due to cave-ins and other hazards. Instead of dragging the bodies out, they buried them in the walls."

Another short yelp echoed from behind, closer this time.

"So, this place is haunted," Henrik concluded as the tunnel bent in the opposite direction.

"That's the consensus," Callan answered.

"Remind me to ask you more thorough questions before you take us anywhere," Henrik remarked. While Joss would have laughed at the comment, she was more in agreement.

It didn't help that a section of the lights was out in this part, all three bracing themselves as they hurried along. Another tunnel came into view, this one wheezing as if there was an opening in the distance they couldn't see. It reminded them of someone unable to breathe, as if being suffocated, or buried alive. When the tunnel straightened out, Callan broke out into a jog, the other two following just as hurriedly.

Finally, the ending came into view, a rickety ladder pushed up against the impacted wall.

"Should one of us go first?" Joss offered, but Callan was already hauling himself up the ladder. Coming up behind, she found nothing but darkness, wondering how high the tunnel went until suddenly she heard Callan grunting as he pushed something out of the way. Slowly, light filtered down, and once Callan moved, all Joss saw was the beginning of the sunset overhead, red-lined clouds drifting by against the deepening blue sky.

The distant knocking chased Joss as she climbed the ladder after him, Henrik right behind. Reaching the top, she peeked her head out, finding the opening was sunken down into the ground with overgrown bushes formed all around. Finding a thin slab of stone pushed off to the side, she searched for Callan and found him crawling underneath the bushes. Following him, she crawled a little way before looking back to make sure Henrik was following.

Coming to a clearing, Callan was already standing, brushing himself off as Joss and Henrik came to stand with him. They barely had time to compose themselves when Callan moved forward, disappearing into the plush garden. Trees and thick flower bushes surrounded the area as the castle towered over them, the windows beginning to glow with light for the evening.

Joss gawked at the sight until Henrik tugged on her arm,

pulling her in the direction he saw Callan go. Making their way around aromatic gardenias and multicolored azaleas, they caught up to Callan, finding him stalking around an overgrown shrub of some kind. The two gave chase, but upon reaching him, they skidded to an unexpected stop.

In front of Callan were two guards, a sword strapped to one side of their hip while their pistols were drawn from the holster they wore on the other.

All those days of no one recognizing Callan flooded Joss with cold fear, wondering how they'd make it past them.

"What the hell?" one of the guards was saying. "Your Highness?"

Thank God, Joss sighed, relief overpowering her. Even Henrik's shoulders dropped, feeling the same.

"It's been an awfully long time, Sir Drodd, Sir Gwain," Callan spoke up, nodding to each.

A moment of silence passed before the guard quickly dropped his pistol, falling to his knee, the other guard following suit. "Sir, where have you been?" he asked, rushed, his head still bowed.

"I'll explain later. I have to get to the Great Hall."

Looking up, urgency marred both guards' faces. "Go tell the others." The guard commanded his comrade, who quickly got up, bowed, and ran off. The remaining guard, Sir Drodd, came to his feet, suddenly seeing Joss and Henrik. The three exchanged looks, unsure of each other.

"They're with me," Callan reassured.

Not questioning him, Sir Drodd insisted, "We need to hurry. The council is already here."

CHAPTER EIGHTEEN

Aric's first kill in the tunnel was, more or less, a surprise.

He was meandering through the underground, taking his time. The knocking sounds and airy whispers unnerved him, but he remained on his path, anticipating what was to come, either in front of him or behind. The lights overhead didn't help either, making his nerves race, wondering if he'd be thrown back into complete darkness.

It was when he rounded past another endless corner that he finally came face-to-face with one of the masked goons. By how the figure was hurrying, he must not have liked being down there either.

With both coming to a stop, the two stared at each other before the masked figure went for something at his hip. Assuming it was a gun, Aric darted forward, kicking the man right in the chest which caused him to fall backwards. Hitting the ground, he had just fished out the pistol from his holster when Aric's knee thudded against his chest, pinning him down and causing a scream to erupt, which echoed throughout the tunnel. He didn't have a chance to raise his arm before the blade of the knife sank into his neck, changing his scream into a gurgling noise before the silence took him.

Pulling the blade out, Aric used the man's cloak to clean the knife and lifted the mask up. *Nope, still don't know you*, he thought, letting go of the mask which snapped back onto the man's face.

He was coming to his feet when he heard the voice.

"Let's just say there's a reason why many don't come down here."

While the tone was faint, Aric recognized Callan Ronen's voice immediately.

He made it in, Aric thought. If the prince was down here, then there was a chance Jocelyn and Henrik were too.

Eyeing the gun, Aric decided to leave it. If it went off, anyone in the tunnels would hear it, putting Callan, Jocelyn, and Henrik in danger if any more of those masked cretins were hanging around. Besides, he was used to doing things the quiet way; it was the habit of being an assassin.

He hurried quietly through the tunnel, following it while it curved. Some of the bulbs continued flickering, harsher than before, as he found that his path ended at another tunnel a little way down.

He still heard Callan as he came to the adjoining tunnel, the distant echoes erasing his words but not his tone. Cautiously looking both ways, Aric found only flickering lights in either direction. A knock came from somewhere deep in the walls, but for Aric that's not what had crawled up his spine.

It was the sound of footsteps and rustling coming from behind him.

Sidestepping into the other tunnel and pressing against the wall, he faced the direction Callan's voice had traveled from, waiting poised against the dirt. He heard the footsteps drawing around the bend, coming to the same junction. Aric knelt down, readying himself.

The sound of boot heels against the dirt drew closer, and as the figure rounded the turn, Aric bolted to his feet, shoving the blade straight up into where the man's jaw met his neck. A short yelp escaped the man out of surprise before the blade silenced him, turning any screams into gurgles as Aric shoved him into the wall and stabbed him again for good measure. Once the body dropped to the ground, Aric wiped the blade and his hands on the man's cloak, knowing the blood would soon make things sticky for him if he needed to use the knife again.

Aric found himself eyeing the tunnel the man was aiming for. While the curious part of him wanted to see what was over there, the thought of Jocelyn being down the other corridor sent him in her direction. The knocking of the walls trailed after him as he went in pursuit of the woman he owed his life to, hoping that, if the occasion called for it, he could return the favor.

CHAPTER NINETEEN

Muriel's feet felt heavy as she followed the procession towards the Great Hall.

She had been changed into one of her more regal gowns—a flowing black dress overlaid in dark lace. The collar, which matched the fitted belt against her waist that enhanced her figure, wrapped around her neck before draping down across her bodice and around her shoulders. It was pure gold etched in filigree; the metal purposely molded to fit her. The dress was delicately attached to it, and hanging from the metal portion and dropping from her shoulders was a layer of lace a shade lighter than the rest. Even with the gold fitting exposing her shoulders, the lace fabric gave the illusion of a delicate cape that trailed against her dress, sweeping against the ground behind her in a train. They undid her braid, taming the mass of dark curls by fitting a gold headdress on her. It pressed against her forehead before winding around her head, dainty chains of braided gold looping around the base of it and used to help weigh down the wildness of her hair.

She would have looked stunning if the side of her lip and eye wasn't welted from Davien's hand, and her eyes weren't so bloodshot from all the tears. It also didn't help that she hadn't worn the dress in years, causing parts of the metal to dig into her skin. It wasn't the type of dress she would have worn in mourning; but then again, this wasn't a typical situation for her to be in.

"You should have been taking better care of yourself," Charisse had hissed, entering at the exact time the ladies-in-waiting were fitting Muriel's corset, tugging hard. The ladies had already changed into their black attire, hurried along by Davien's knights who made sure no one was lingering around for too long.

Besides the knights, Charisse had arrived to make sure Muriel was cooperating, most likely at Davien's request. Her own ladies-in-waiting were missing, as they had been since Charisse hadn't left the king's side in days. Despite their absence, however she too was wearing black, but a much simpler version compared to what she normally wore, a sign that they had to work extra quickly so Charisse could be present in Muriel's chambers. The grief was visible, burned into her eyes that constantly blurred with tears. Trying to remain strong, the tears were what softened her, making her harshest stare a little less poignant. Muriel wanted to hate her, but she had to remind herself that Charisse had just lost her husband. In that small moment, both queen and princess were pained by the same agony.

With teeth gritted and tears staining her cheeks, Muriel had remained placid. Her ladies hurried to fit and adorn her, the finishing touches being the gold drop earrings and the two gold bracelets that they snapped onto her wrists like shackles. Her wedding ring was absent, thanks to a loud glare from Charisse. Muriel didn't have a chance to hide the cloth with Callan's words on it, but thankfully the lady-in-waiting who found it didn't say anything, only exchanged a look with Muriel before keeping it in her hands, hidden away.

Now, with two guards in front, her stepmother-in-law next to her, and her ladies-in-waiting trailing behind, Muriel walked in a fog, only following the motion because she knew it so well. Callan should have arrived by now, but with the king dead, there would only be one way to claim the throne once Davien was crowned, and that's if Davien hadn't gotten to her husband first.

I'll kill you, she thought as they passed corridor after corridor, the chandeliers spilling light across the detailed halls. The elegant mirrors cast back her beautiful reflection that stood out against all the other colors which made the castle so ornate.

Muriel had never harmed anything in her life—thought about it plenty of times but never actually acted—but once Davien's hand struck her face in the dead king's chambers, she realized her time was up. He had won, he'd have her, and she'd have to make a choice: give into him or do what no one else had been able to.

You'll have to sleep sometime, prince. Her mind twisted as she imagined bludgeoning him to death with one of those heavy candlesticks, or stabbing him with his own dagger. The thought of spending the night with him made her stomach curl, but if he was going to win this round, fine; she'd destroy him in the next. And once they realized it was her and she was taken to the gallows as a murderess, she'd smile. She'd smile because in the end—no matter what he did or said, no matter what laws forced her hand in his—

she'd always be Callan's wife. Not even God would be able to tell her otherwise.

Poisoning Davien as an alternative method had come to mind just before Muriel saw the massive doors which led into the Great Hall, Davien and his knights standing ready before them.

Anxiety twisted itself into her gut, sitting so heavily inside her that it made it hard to breathe. The corset didn't help either, causing her sides to ache, her chest to tighten, her skin to burn. The flash of anger came quickly, heating up her face as she was ushered forward, Davien's smug look becoming clear as she was forced to stand behind him. Charisse remained next to her, and while Muriel refused to make eye contact with anyone, she noticed that among the men, Eiden wasn't there.

Feeling her throat go dry, Muriel cringed as the massive doors split open, widening before them. She could see the chandeliers overhead, the pillars stretching from the first floor to the second, breaking the balconies into a scalloped fashion that wrapped around the room, allowing viewers to look down on what was happening below. Despite the balconies' reach, the sconces were all turned off, causing the second floor to fall into an empty darkness while the chandeliers' lights were focused on the main floor.

This is being done quickly, Muriel realized, the rush of the day catching up to her.

Davien drew forward then, and Muriel was forced to follow on his left, Charisse keeping step with her on his right. The ladies-in-waiting followed behind, and when Muriel looked behind her shoulder, she found Davien's knights trailing last. Still, there was no Eiden.

The youngest must have been at a brothel, Muriel was rationalizing, wondering how upset he'd be that this procession was happening without him. Knowing Eiden, he wouldn't care. The chances of him being king were slim, especially when growing up with two older brothers. He never took his duties seriously, anyway.

Despite the rationalization, Muriel marked it as one more thing that made Davien so hateful. It wasn't surprising he'd leave his youngest brother out. Less competition; less chances of someone calling out Mors Exitus on him.

Davien led the procession line to the center of the room where a group of men stood milling around before the doors had opened. Now, they were all bowed on one knee, welcoming the future king. From where Muriel was, she could see it was the council, except for a couple knights who remained off to the side, holding an engraved wooden box. They had clearly been summoned separately.

Coming to a stop a short distance away, Davien told them to rise. "Gentlemen, thank you for coming," he proceeded, trying to sound calm despite the anticipation setting in by how he stretched out his hand at his side. "As you've heard the bells, it is with great sorrow that I relay the message of the passing of our great king and my dear father, King Lyson Ronen."

The solemn faces of the council foretold they already knew, given how the bells had gone off and they were all summoned. However, the shock was still evident among them, as if no one thought the king would actually die, or that it would be Davien who would take his place. For the first time, Muriel was confronted with the fact that many of them had been holding out hope for

Callan, given the same disappointment in their expressions when they glanced at her.

One of the older council members stepped forward, and in his somberness, he turned, able to view both the royal family and the rest of the council. The knights with the box stepped forward, facing him.

"May the reign of King Lyson Ronen of Aselian forever be remembered as a prosperous one," the councilman spoke. "Prosperous in courage, prosperous in honesty, prosperous in all the ways that made him a good king." The councilman cleared his throat before adding, "May we all be forever in his favor just as he was in ours."

There was a hesitation, but with a curt nod from Davien, the knight pulled back the lid of the box. As if begrudgingly, the councilman stepped closer to the box and lifted the crown from its resting spot. It glistened in the light, the gold and burgundy jewels twinkling as he looked to the councilmen. With no one interjecting, the councilman rotated to stand in front of Davien. Muriel couldn't see the prince's face, but by how much he straightened up, she pressed her lips together so she wouldn't scream in rage. Instead, tears fell down her cheeks as she squeezed her eyes shut, unable to stomach the sight.

"As God is our witness, in front of royal and common alike," the councilman's voice boomed, raising the crown up high so everyone could see it. "We, the people of Aselian, anoint you, Prince Davien Ronen, as king and sovereign of this kingdom. May your reign be blessed and prosperous, and may you bring peace to our realm that others have strived for."

Silence followed, the crown lowering quietly onto Davien's head. The councilman's mouth remained a grim line as he removed his hands and stepped back. "Long live our new sovereign, King Davien Ronen of Aselian."

"Long live the king" rippled through the group, joined in by the ladies-in-waiting and knights. The only one who didn't reply was Muriel, who kept her lips pinched shut as the chorus rose around her.

Another round of "long live the king" echoed into the room, but it was during the third and final round that another voice—louder and harsher—interrupted them.

"MORS EXITUS!"

The chant died instantly, all heads turning to the far door that had opened without them knowing. The voice shook Muriel awake, and upon seeing the figure, her mouth dropped, a gasp escaping.

Other gasps and murmurs broke throughout the small crowd, his name slipping from their lips as the man marched into the room, no one noticing the woman and lad who followed behind him. All eyes were on *him*: his stature that mimicked his father, his features, which were recognizable even after so many years, and his grip on the sword that was ready and waiting.

Callan Ronen had finally come home.

CHAPTER TWENTY

The inside of the castle was about as overwhelming as the outside, and it took everything in Joss to keep her focus on keeping up with the prince. The way the frosted glass in the sconces and chandeliers spilled an ambient light into the rooms and halls made the place even more heavenly. The gilded mirrors and scenic portraits, along with the adorned rugs and furnishings, were all so regal that Joss had to force herself to ignore it just to keep up with Callan, who stormed the castle at a run.

Despite the beauty, Joss felt the anxiety in her chest, the anticipation of what would happen causing her skin to prickle. It chased after her as she followed them, the ax heavy in hand, a reminder she wasn't powerless, she could hold her own. Granted, this wasn't Galmoor and there were too many guards and knights present with both guns and blades at their disposal. But Joss had worked in a jailhouse for a good portion of her life, and the desperation in some of those feral prisoners had taught her how to use the ax in more ways than just executing.

Up the stairs, past balconies overlooking sitting rooms, corridors opening into spaces with no use except to highlight its own beauty, the group ran. Despite the armor, Sir Drodd stayed in stride with Callan while Joss and Henrik trailed after. Finally, they approached two massive doors. Before Sir Drodd opened one of them, Callan asked for his sword.

Knowing full well what it meant, the knight did what he was told, and Callan handed him the revolver. There was no look back, no last words, as the knight pulled the door open and Callan moved in, sword in hand. The knight held the door open for Joss and Henrik before slipping in behind them.

The room was about as majestic as the rest of the place. Joss took note of the balconies overhead, finding only darkness when her eyes lowered, settling on the group of men in the center of the room, chanting "Long live the king."

"MORS EXITUS!"

Callan's voice shook her as she slowed herself to a walk to assess the situation, Henrik remaining with her as both watched all heads turn to see Callan. Gasps and murmurs erupted, and the group of men parted, revealing the newly crowned king. Joss recognized Davien from earlier, Muriel standing behind him with a group mixed of men and women, all wearing some form of black mourning apparel.

"I witness it!" Joss yelled out, remembering the rules, and Henrik yelled, "I second it!"

The men who parted—the councilmen, Joss figured—had backed away on either side. Even the men and women behind the royal family did the same, wanting to get out of the way now that

Mors Exitus was in play.

"Callan!" Muriel cried out. She had just rounded past Davien when he clutched her wrist and whipped her back against him. She struggled until the revolver touched her jaw, causing her to stop.

"One more step, brother!" Davien warned.

Joss tugged at Henrik's arm, pulling him to a stop as Callan took a couple more steps before finally halting, the words sinking in slowly thanks to his anger.

"I declared Mors Exitus," Callan called back. "Let her go!"

"And I was declared king," Davien replied, laughing a little. "And now she's mine. All of it is mine!"

"Only if I don't kill you," Callan reminded him, pointing the sword in his direction. "Which, I assure you, brother, fate will not be in your favor."

"Fate or not, you will not win!" Davien promised, pressing the steel into Muriel's jaw so hard it distorted her face, her mouth open and sideways, tears streaming down her cheeks and chin.

"Muriel," Callan whispered harshly, unable to hold back her name now that she was in front of him.

"Callan," she responded, "kill him!"

Her head snapped back by how Davien grabbed her hair, causing a sharp scream to erupt.

"Davien!" someone hissed out, and an older woman who was also dressed in mourning clothes stepped forward from where she had been guided off to the side. "This isn't you," she reminded him, the tone that of a mother's.

"You don't know me!" Davien snapped.

"He declared Mors Exitus," she reminded him. "You have to

follow the laws—"

"Fuck the laws!" Davien screamed, his body jerking and causing another yelp from Muriel. "I've waited *years* for this! I stayed while he abandoned us! Do none of you remember?"

He searched the room, but no one else stepped forward.

"You are dishonoring our bloodline," the older woman said back, though it was obvious the words were hard to say. "At least let her go. This is between you and your brother now."

"Listen to her," Callan pressed, taking a slight step forward.

"She's only saying that because you are your father's son," Davien spit out, the jealousy evident in his glare.

"She's saying it because *you* are *her* son," Callan reminded him. "Let my wife go and fight me like a man."

Davien's head shook, taking a step back.

"Fight me!" Callan demanded.

As Callan drew closer and Davien fell back, Joss held onto Henrik's arm, keeping him where they were. She noticed something on the balcony, thinking she saw a shadow up there in the dimness. It wasn't until the massive doors at the other end slightly opened and a figure emerged that Joss felt the tension press into her. By how Henrik's breath caught, he too saw the figure.

"Fight me, you coward!" Callan demanded again, evident that his sole attention was on Davien.

"You're not going to win this!" Davien screamed back, pulling Muriel along with him, who was using both her hands to try to get his hand to release her hair.

"You've wanted me dead this whole time, yet you still can't do it yourself. Even hiring an assassin was cowardly," Callan was growling.

"Assassin," he breathed out, clearly confused. "What assassin?"

The gunshot answered him, and Davien's body instantly stiffened before he fell forward. The crown toppled from his head, landing with a loud *clink* before it came to rest by him. The spray of blood still lingered in the air after his body hit the floor.

Joss covered her mouth, hearing the screams fill the air as Muriel fell with him, revealing the hooded figure who fired the pistol from behind, a charcoal-grey mask hiding his face. Callan went to catch her before the pistol was aimed at him, forcing him to a halt.

Muriel crawled away from Davien's body, her dress ripping as she tried to get to her feet. One of the councilmen rushed over, helping her up, but then another shot was fired, hitting the ground by them and sending them running to the side. More shots were fired as men—knights, it looked like, despite the fact they weren't wearing armor like the one that escorted them in—tried reaching for their guns, some succeeding, some failing. A couple successfully shot back, and the masked figure flinched as a bullet struck him.

It's him, Joss realized, remembering that same figure in the doorway of the tavern in Raspshire; how Callan fired at him with his own pistol, and he hadn't fallen.

The accuracy of the masked figure was overwhelming, and within seconds, the knights who tried for him were on the ground, their blood pooling around them. The rest of the groups on either side of the room huddled together, crouched on the ground covered under the balconies.

Joss caught movement to the side. Sir Drodd moved to take

aim but thought better of it after seeing what happened to the other men. He remained near one of the groups, the revolver in hand as he surveyed the area, keeping to his duties.

The only one who remained standing was Callan, along with Joss and Henrik who remained a few paces behind. The older woman—Davien's mother—had thrown herself to her fallen son, crying as she laid across him, a mother to the end.

"Run for the door," Henrik whispered, pulling Joss from the scene.

Before Joss could reply, the room echoed from the banging on the massive doors from both ends. The noise startled everyone, causing more screams to erupt from the women and a couple of the men. It took a small moment for the realization to hit: the doors were now blocked on the other side, keeping them trapped in the Great Hall.

"Well, well," the muffled voice spoke out, holding the gun up. "The prodigal son has returned," he announced.

Callan didn't reply. From where she stood, Joss could tell Davien's last words were still hanging in the air. He hadn't sent Aric after him; he wasn't the one who betrayed Callan in those little towns, among his own men.

That only left one other person, the only royal who wasn't in the room.

"You must be the Mask," Callan surmised.

"I'm glad you've heard of me." The Mask seemed to smile. "It makes our introductions much simpler."

"About as simple as it was to kill your own brother while his back was turned."

The Mask stopped then, eyeing Callan.

"All that training and you still didn't learn much," Callan continued, "did you, Eiden?"

A moment of silence lapsed before the chuckling started, filling the space with an amused laugh. Slowly, the Mask drew his hood off, and then pulled the mask off.

The gasps filling the room told Joss that Callan was right.

"Don't be mad, brother," Eiden smiled. "I only did what you couldn't."

"You're right. Being dishonorable isn't my forte," Callan confronted.

"It never was; hence, your current dilemma." Eiden pointed the pistol at him again, causing a whimper to escape from Muriel, still being held back by one of the councilmen.

Joss felt that whimper as if it had touched her bones, and the aching it triggered caused her to gasp a little, not realizing she had been holding her breath. She had heard heartache before while on the gallows, but this one got to her. Knowing Callan made it personal, and the reunion they should have had in the garden still glistened in Joss's mind, a happily ever after in a world full of suffering. She hadn't seen that kind of happiness in an awfully long time, and hearing Muriel's fear only solidified how unfair the world was.

"So, you were behind everything," Callan was speaking out, accusing yet bewildered. "Sir Percy's betrayal. My imprisonment. The assassination attempt. It was all because of you."

"You never did give me enough credit," Eiden pointed out.

"You knew?" The older woman slowly rose to her feet, now

standing in the open space between Callan and Eiden, her other son lying at her feet.

"Charisse, don't," Callan warned, a hand lifting, wanting to stop her.

"You knew he was alive this whole time?" Charisse asked, her tone laced with disgust.

"I know a lot of things, mother," Eiden corrected her, the gun still raised. "That's the beauty of being underestimated."

The anger was evident by how her fists trembled. "His father should have been told," she growled.

Eiden laughed lightly. "And do you think that would have prolonged his life a little more?"

Charisse glared at him, cold regalness eclipsing the sorrow. "I didn't raise my sons to be like this," she lamented.

Eiden's laugh fell into a smirk. "Of course you didn't, mother. We did this all on our own."

The shot fired was as alarming as watching Charisse's body fall to the floor.

Screams erupted, but not as loud as Callan's. "What the fuck is wrong with you!" he bellowed, his anger flaring.

"A lot of things," Eiden admitted, his cool composure a stark contrast to his brother's hot rage. "The most important one being how much I despise this entire realm and all the people in it."

Eiden swept a hand around the room, as if everyone there had already proven his point. Joss couldn't help but follow his gesture, seeing how they all were cowering, realizing the threat extended far past the royal family.

"Then why the hell are you here?" Callan questioned, gripping the sword in response when Eiden checked his pistol, finding the chamber empty.

Tossing the weapon, Eiden made his way back to one of the fallen knights. Just as he passed, one of the councilmen rose, a hidden pistol in hand. From where Joss stood, standing back and watching the entire scene unfold, she wasn't sure where he got the gun from, unless he had had it on him the entire time. As the man raised the weapon, the room holding its breath, anticipating the end of this terrible scene, something shot through the air from the second-floor balcony above. The man grunted, his body jolting as an arrow stuck out of his chest. As he fell back, one of the other members caught him, lowering him to the ground as he grunted and moaned from the sudden attack.

"Because." Eiden seemed to laugh, unfazed by the whole ordeal as if expecting it. He was pulling out the dead knight's sword, testing its grip as he made his way to the center of the room. Eyeing the councilman with the arrow, he smirked before he leveled his gaze back on Callan. "Between both of us, I'm the change this place needs."

"You're more like a poison," Callan remarked, unable to hide his disgust.

Eiden laughed, finding it funny. "Oh, come on, now. Everyone here knows Davien couldn't rule. He couldn't even *try* to fight you. And mother? She was always too infatuated with our old man. She'd do anything in her power to make sure his legacy continued way past his death, not giving a shit about our own.

"And you." Eiden pointed the sword at Callan as he began to slowly approach. "You're just like him: traditional, stuffy. You bend to old rules that no longer fit our society."

"And you think people will willingly follow you after what you've done?" Callan pointed out, acknowledging the fallen bodies, blood still pooling on the floor.

"I can be persuasive," Eiden smiled, a hand sweeping over to the man who laid against his counterpart, the arrow causing his breath to become labored. "And now everyone here now knows that," he called out, as if daring someone else to step forward.

No one did.

"But I know you, brother," Eiden continued, twisting the sword around in his hand as if playing. "You came for a fight, and a fight you shall have."

Callan readied himself, his body immediately falling into his warrior stance. "Let's see how much you actually learned," he growled.

The smashing of the blades as the swords collided gave him his answer.

CHAPTER TWENTY-ONE

It could have been the fatigue, the days spent riding hard to get home. It could have been the years spent as a prisoner of war, beaten and starved, the abuse reaching as deep as his psyche. It could easily have been his anger, rage blinding years of instructions and discipline. Or even just grief, knowing that once he killed his brother, his entire family would be gone, including the father he never got to say goodbye to.

No matter the real cause, Callan Ronen was losing.

A sweep of the blade caught the side of his leg, leaving a trail of blood as he stumbled to the right, regaining his balance. A wrong turn landed the hilt of the sword to his face. A punch to the back of his shoulder caused a loud growl to erupt, a reaction to a wound that was already there but forgotten—the leftover mark of an assassin's arrow.

After a swift dance, the ramming of Eiden's fist into Callan's rib cage caused him to stagger back, the air rushing out of his lungs. He still was able to catch most of Eiden's blows and tried to deal them back, but the younger man was just a step quicker, blocking each strike he dealt. A couple of times Callan sliced across his rib cage and abdomen, but the sword slipped by without leaving a mark except for the torn shirt, the only sign the blade had touched him. The leather vest blocked the rest of the attack.

Everyone watched helplessly, afraid of both Callan falling and the threats hidden above them on the balconies. Joss, however, was watching Eiden; how he struck, how he moved. He was fluid and elegant, making it look all too easy. While Callan had those same attributes, something was anchoring the lost prince down. Fatigue, anger, or grief; something was getting in the way.

"If you're such a magnificent fighter, why didn't you come after me yourself?" Callan questioned, trying to buy some time as he shook off the pains in his body.

"Why, when I have others who can do it for me?" Eiden shrugged before nodding to the man with the arrow embedded in him. "Granted, I wanted less people involved so there'd be less blunders—and I was really hoping the war would just do you in— but nay, here you are, ruining things as usual."

"I never disappoint," Callan remarked back. "Besides, I see you're making good use of my vest," he pointed out as he sucked in deep breaths, trying to hide the panting.

"It's an ingenious invention. Too bad you don't want to join me, give me more tips," Eiden remarked, swiping his sword and causing Callan to land on his knee, ducking. "If you weren't so much your father's son, you'd be impressed by the plans we have."

Callan gritted his teeth, trying to get back into stance, even though he was limping now. "*We?*" he hissed out.

"Myself and my new ally, once I'm officially crowned." Eiden smiled, lunging at Callan who blocked the attack. Blades smashed in a rhythm before both brothers separated, anticipating the next attack. They had moved towards the other door, causing Henrik and Joss to back out of the way, watching from underneath the balcony. While their attention remained on the fight, Joss glanced up at the balconies across the way, seeing movements in the shadows but unable to see what they were.

"And who the hell would that be?" Callan questioned, his heavy breathing becoming more pronounced. His stance was collapsing, his shoulders rounding over from the pain in his body.

Eiden began to back up, crossing the room as if to gain everyone's attention, which he did, including Joss.

"We have a history of making friends with powerful allies," Eiden was saying, coming to stand in the center of the room.

"Correnth is already an ally," Callan spoke up, announcing what everyone already knew: the kingdom of Correnth was the most powerful ally they had, the only other kingdom who held the mountain pass against the barbarians.

Joss looked across the room at him, soaking in the political schemes that were bubbling up. While she hadn't kept up with court politics, Galmoor was a town that saw a lot of the aftermath of what the border wars were doing. Correnth's unexpected absence as of late was being felt past the border wars and into the towns. If something was happening with Correnth, then who would take their place?

Eiden chuckled, and that's when Callan's face changed from suspicion to horror. "You wouldn't," he murmured, though still audible given the depth of the room.

"Bellumortis's technology is advancing," Eiden pointed out. "We'd be foolish not to join them. We'd have no more enemies if they were on our side."

There was a rush of murmurs, and even Joss was stunned by the words. Bellumortis wasn't mentioned often, but what she overheard made her think that they weren't a kingdom anyone wanted to associate with. However, she never gave it much thought because most of what she overheard had sounded so outlandish that she figured it was just people running off with their imaginations. The weaponry, the use of chemicals—it couldn't have been true.

"We'd be dead," Callan growled, snapping the tension in the room. "Do you understand what they do to their own people? Don't you think they'd do the same to us?"

"See, this is what's wrong with this place," Eiden balked. "No one wants to see what the future holds. No one wants to examine the potential of something new."

"A future with them will come at a price," Callan barked, but his eyes showed he was pleading. While Joss couldn't account for the rest, the statement about what Bellumortis did to their own people hung in the air like a noose, the fate of Aselian being next.

Eiden's smile remained firm. "Everything comes at a price."

Joss quietly undid the leather pouch on the blade of her ax, so quietly that even Henrik didn't notice, too caught up in the scene.

"Don't forget our motto, brother," Eiden continued, tapping his bicep, the exact area where his tattoo was, matching Callan's; the one given to all who graduated with their training. "Carpe Omnia," he exclaimed proudly. "Seize it all!"

Callan couldn't combat that, though the saying meant something different to him. It was a war cry, a way to boost their spirits in time of battle. It wasn't meant to be used in politics, in power-hungry schemes.

Callan blinked a couple times, realizing it wasn't just the crown in jeopardy now. "You plan to sacrifice our own people, then? For power?"

"If that's what it takes," Eiden quipped. "Nothing good ever came without a little sacrifice."

"You're just as sadistic as they are," Callan remarked as he readied himself, needing to end this fight.

"Call me whatever you want, but I'm not the one bleeding all over the floor." Eiden nodded to the bodies, but not before he took in the wounds he had inflicted already on Callan.

An intense pause came before the blades clashed again, brother against brother. A few gasps pierced the air from the audience around them, seeing Callan tiring faster than his opponent. He fought through the pain and grunts, but then Eiden struck his leg with his boot, and his entire world came crashing down to his knees, his sword flung from his grasp. As he bent up to get it, Eiden laid his blade across the back of his neck, freezing him in place.

"This is the end, brother," Eiden remarked, his heavy breaths foretelling that Callan had at least put up a good fight.

Callan's face twisted from anger to anguish, his gaze falling on Muriel, who was sobbing into her hands. Something in him was scheming, trying to find a way out of this predicament, but his gaze showed he didn't know how.

"Give father my condolences," Eiden smiled, repositioning the blade so the tip was aimed right for Callan's neck.

"Mors Exitus!"

Eiden stopped, and all eyes—even Callan's—came to rest on Joss.

She had stepped forward, ax in hand, the steel glistening from the light of the chandeliers.

"What are you doing?" Henrik hissed behind her, realizing too late that she had a plan.

"Stay where you are," she said back before laughter broke into the room.

Eiden, whose laughter showed his amusement, remained poised behind his brother. "Why, if it isn't Master Joss Brevyn," he mused, his voice rising as if he were introducing her. "The Town Executioner of Galmoor. You couldn't kill him when you were supposed to, so you're deciding to do your duties now?"

"My fight is with you," Joss called back, taking a couple steps forward. Her eyes raised to the balcony, but finding no threats, she lowered her gaze back to the younger prince. "I fight on behalf of Callan Ronen."

Her gaze met Callan, who was shaking his head at her. Ignoring him, she was met with an amused smile from his captor.

"You want to fight me," Eiden repeated, as if he hadn't heard her right. "Darling, I'm not the type of man you've dealt with before."

Joss's gaze swept over the murdered bodies littering the floor and then back to Eiden, his arrogance showing in his smile. It was an expression she had seen all her life through many different faces, usually behind bars or standing on the gallows. "Actually," she corrected him, "you're exactly the type of man I've dealt with."

"Unfortunately, there are rules—"

"I witness it," Henrik spoke up, causing Joss to look at him. Fear sharpened the look in his eyes, but the trust was there speaking for him. "Don't die," he mouthed to her, eyes glistening. All Joss could do was nod in reassurance, though both knew it wasn't guaranteed.

Eiden breathed in, caught between a laugh and disgust. "Are you serious—"

"I second it!" Muriel shouted, rising from where she had been held, her defiance sending her to her feet.

"Alright, then," Eiden replied. "If that's how everyone wants to be." Before walking away, he drew the sword quickly across Callan's bicep, sending the prince into a seething scream. He fell sideways onto the floor, holding his arm with blood gushing from in between his fingers.

"Did you ever come up with an answer to the question?" Eiden asked, walking mildly forward, passing the bodies of his brother and mother without even a glance.

Joss made her way to the middle of the room, coming to face him. "What question?" she asked.

"The question the old man gave you," Eiden replied, coming to a stop while leaving a good distance between them. "Remember, on the gallows? That whole spiel about how 'they made you into what you are,' and '*This* does not define you. You may die a town executioner, but what are you really?'"

Charleston Ore.

Her throat tightened in memory of that conversation with the old thief before she beheaded him. Eiden had been there; the Mask was watching her the entire time. He had been so close; close enough to hear without her knowing it.

They know who you are, what you do. She still heard Aric's words on that ledge, and if she allowed herself, could still feel his hold on her arms, the way he had looked down at her. *They seem to have a lot of eyes around this place...*

"He was right, you know."

Joss blinked, taken aback by the comment.

"They did make you into what you are." Eiden nodded to Callan who remained seething on the ground in the distance. "But I can do better. I can give you what you want."

"You don't know what I want," Joss replied, readying herself.

"Oh, I do," Eiden smiled. "I've seen all the requests for pardons. And I know for a fact that no matter how this ends, if my brother becomes king, he will follow in his father's footsteps and keep you in your position. He never intended to pardon you, even after everything you've done for him."

Joss stared back, keeping her emotions to herself. She had become good at it, even when the words hurt, even when the truth was hard to face.

"Here, let me show you." Eiden put a finger up, as if telling her to wait. He backtracked to Callan, lifting his brother up to his knees, who groaned from his arm.

"Tell her, brother," Eiden coaxed, holding the sword across his neck. "Tell her that if she kills me, then she'll be pardoned. Tell her that she and her assistant can go home fully discharged of their duties."

Callan was breathing hard despite the sword pressing against his throat. He stared back at Joss, something torn on his face.

Joss looked at him, realizing Eiden—the Mask—had been right about everything.

"Go on," Eiden tried again, his smile lighting up his face at the accuracy of his prediction. "Pardon her."

Joss swallowed hard at Callan's silence. He had squeezed his eyes shut from the pain, unwilling to say things he didn't mean. But when he finally opened his eyes, he looked like he did on the gallows when she was about to hang him: his teeth clenched, his dark eyes looking at her, holding both anger and hopelessness.

"Master Brevyn," Eiden sneered, gaining her attention. "You still want to fight for *this*?"

Turning her gaze to Henrik, she found the lad staring wide-eyed at the scene. He wasn't standing next to her like he normally did, but he was still there, sharing the same fate. And while a part of her was wondering what to do, Henrik locked eyes with her. Something passed between them, and he nodded, the same type of nod she had given him when she silently told him that she was going to save the prince. He hadn't questioned her then, and he wasn't questioning her now. He never did.

Looking back at Eiden, Joss replied in the same calm way she did when confronting an antagonizing prisoner. "Yes, I do."

There was barely a look of surprise in Callan's gaze as Eiden shoved his brother to the side, striking him on the side of the face with the hilt of his sword. Callan fell to the ground, a gash on his temple with blood already dripping down the side of his face.

While he tried to remain conscious, still holding his arm, it was obvious that he was dazed.

"So that's the answer to the question," Eiden remarked, circling around Joss, who followed by pivoting her steps to remain facing him. "Once a deathsman, always a deathsman."

CHAPTER TWENTY-TWO

For the first time that day, Aric wished he had brought his crossbow.

He had followed the ladder up from the tunnels, crawling through the underbrush and coming out into the garden. He rounded past the thick overlay of foliage, using the shrubbery as cover. He even made it into the castle, using the cover of shadows to lean into the dark corners hiding him from passing guards. What he didn't expect was that some of the guards—knights cleared from war to protect the royal family—weren't all one in the same. The traditional guards were dressed in full armor, swords and pistols strapped to their hips for whatever occasion called for it. But the others seemed... off. They weren't fully dressed in armor, despite the way they patrolled around. And they weren't rushing into duty, hadn't joined in the flurry of putting the castle into lockdown because the Prince Royal had returned to claim his birthright. These knights looked lost, panicked; as if they had been training for a battle they never thought would come.

It was obvious they didn't work for the royal family. They were working for someone else.

Seeing one of these so-called knights coming down the corridor, Aric figured he'd test out the situation, because, in all honesty, why not?

"Callan Ronen is alive," he called out, stopping the knight in his tracks. He looked like a deer that was spooked, completely alarmed. And then suddenly, his gaze hardened, and he drew out his sword.

Not the pistol. Interesting, Aric thought, observing the man who was now storming towards him. All the knight had to do was pull out the gun, or call for his comrades, and the fight would be over. And Aric would have just aimed his crossbow and ended it before it began. It seemed both men had chosen the harder way to fight.

A quick sweep of the sword, a couple shuffles of feet, and Aric had the knife sticking into the man's forearm. Hearing the sword escape his grasp, Aric tripped the man, following him to the ground. With his knee on his chest, he hovered the knife over the man's neck as the knight tried to block it with his good hand.

"Who do you fight for?" Aric asked, staring the knight down.

"The crown," the man growled back.

There were at least three people who could hold that title, Aric realized. "Which crown?" he tried to pinpoint.

The knight stared at him. Suddenly, Aric felt the man's other hand grip his wrist. With one quick jab, the man used Aric's hand to puncture the blade into his own throat.

Confused, Aric watched him bleed out, his eyes fluttering until finally nothing was left.

"Fine, keep your secret," he mumbled, pulling the blade out and cleaning it on the man's sleeve.

Rising, he went in the opposite direction of the entrance. It was touch and go, dodging runaway knights and having to hurry up staircases without being seen. He was halfway up when the sudden shout caused him to miss a step.

"Move aside!"

Aric crouched down, realizing the voice was up at the top of the stairs where the Great Hall was. Slinking up the steps, Aric raised himself enough to find the group of knights standing in front of the door. One of them moved away, running off, and that's when Aric saw the hooded figures they were standing off against, dark masks in place of their faces. Across the massive doors to the Great Hall was a wooden beam, blocking anyone from going in or out.

That's new, he thought as some of the knights drew their swords, the others behind them keeping their hands on their pistols as backup.

"The king is dead," a muffled voice protruded from one of the hooded figures. "We will not move until our true leader is crowned."

"Our true leader is Callan Ronen," the knight growled, "who's come home."

As if on cue, each of the hooded figures stepped into a kind of half-circle, producing a pistol in either hand, aiming them at the knights. By the show of weapons, the knights were outgunned, causing them to hesitate.

"Callan Ronen will be dead soon as well," the muffled voice

finished, revealing they were one step ahead of them.

Jocelyn might be in there, Aric's mind screamed, causing him to quietly backtrack to a servant's corridor on the other side of the staircase. Knowing about the second floor, Aric went deeper into the servant's hall, racing along the narrow pathway and up the staircases, finding them abandoned. He had used these halls before, had been up there on those balconies countless times. Normally, he would have run into at least one servant, but given the timing of the king's death, the servant's halls were abandoned. They had obviously been pulled elsewhere, given that a dead king lay behind these walls. Aric followed it by memory until finally he came to a hooded figure guarding the hallway.

Aric was already running full speed, rounding a corner when he ran into him. By the time he caught sight of the mask, he had already thrown his elbow into the face, smashing the mask and throwing the figure backwards. A flip of the knife caused the blade to sink into the man's clavicle, and Aric followed the man down to the floor. Ripping the mask off, Aric gawked at the young face staring back, a lad who looked to be in his late teen years.

He's too young, Aric thought, pulling the boy's sleeve up. He checked the inside of his bicep, finding no tattoo. No wonder he had been easy to kill; he didn't know how to fight well yet.

As Aric looked him over, he realized that the boy must have been in his first year of training, recruited to be an easy casualty when need be.

"Please," the boy whispered, and Aric saw that he wasn't begging to live.

The assassin didn't think twice when he sunk the blade in again, making sure the boy bled out faster to give him a quicker death.

A little shaken by the unexpected youth, Aric moved on, finding the stairwell he needed. His footsteps fell away until he stopped at the entrance, peering in.

All the sconces were unlit, the only light being the chandeliers hovering over the first floor, which left quite a bit of the second floor in shadows. The balconies were rounded, floating over the edges of the floor below and creating a scalloped-like pattern all the way around the room. Every few feet were rounded marble pillars stretching from floor to ceiling, breaking up each balcony into its own section with a golden, intricately carved railing to hold back the onlookers.

The memories flooded him then; the masquerades he had watched, being perched in the shadows of this very same balcony, overlooking the floor below at all the swirls of color and eyeless sockets that made the court the most interesting thing in his life. It was still there, that little ache of missing the splendor, the drama, the ability to be easily anonymous and play any part he wished.

But then he heard voices drifting from the bottom floor, followed by the echo of clashing steel, which flung him back to reality.

There was movement in the far corner, and he caught the side of an archer, hooded and poised with his bow and arrow, his quiver on his back filled to the brim. Scouring the area, Aric caught sight of the others, pressing themselves into the shadows. Only one looked up across the way, revealing the dark mask he wore.

Again, Aric wished he had brought his crossbow.

CHAPTER TWENTY-THREE

The first swing came unexpectedly, but Joss was used to the unexpected, blocking the attack with the side of her ax that left the clashing sound of steel to pierce the air. The force caused her hand to hurt, which she shook out briefly before gripping the ax again.

"Pivot!" Callan called out from the ground, just as Eiden swung again.

Joss turned, his blade only catching air. A couple of people gasped, audible through the hush that fell into the room.

"Funny you should help her," Eiden called back, "since you couldn't do it yourself."

"Eiden, leave her out of this," one of the councilmen was saying, someone trying to reason the situation. Another answered for him, restating the rules of Mors Exitus, which quieted any other objections.

Callan, however, either hadn't heard or didn't care. "Your fight is with me, Eiden!" he yelled out, that demanding tone filling the air. Out of the corner of her eye, Joss saw Callan rising to his knees, still clutching his arm.

"Don't worry, I haven't forgotten," Eiden laughed before lunging at Joss, the sword blocked by the ax blade.

It was obvious he was toying with her, for reasons Joss wasn't sure. But then again, she was doing the same thing. If she could get a good couple of wounds in, then she might be able to level the playing field for Callan. He was bad off though, and her mind kept trailing back to the cut on his arm, knowing it needed to be fixed or he would lose more blood and be rendered useless. His leg was cut too, but the cut on his arm looked deeper.

Dodging another blow, Joss called out to no one in particular, "Tie his arm! You must stop the bleeding!"

Eiden cut the blade into the air, which Joss caught with the ax. Instead of breaking away, Eiden kept the sword pressed against her blade, the momentum pushing Joss back a couple steps.

"Always trying to be a healer, aren't you?" he remarked, staring at her as he moved closer, showing his strength by how the sword didn't give way from its position.

"You talk too much," she seethed back, throwing her foot into his knee. The sudden hit caused him to groan as his leg went out, giving Joss a chance to push the sword away with the ax. Backing off, she watched as he regained himself. She knew she should have struck again, but she didn't quite know how to since she had never been the one to attack, only defend.

"No wonder he liked you."

Joss relaxed then tightened her grip, tried to stretch the tension out of her hands as Eiden's groans turned quietly into a type of chuckle. She eyed him as he shook his leg and then walked the pain off, starting to circle her again. It was as he turned that she caught sight of Henrik, inching his way along the wall towards Callan. He made it to the doors, watching the balcony in case someone was taking aim. Her heart quickened as she tried to keep her attention on Eiden, though needing to make sure Henrik made it safely across.

"I hear Aric Kayden was a hard man to impress, and yet you managed it."

Hearing Aric's name used in past reference made something in her falter. She blinked a couple times to keep herself grounded.

"The way he was with those harlots," Eiden continued, whistling at the end of the word. "I'm a little surprised he even considered you."

"Focus," Joss whispered to herself, knowing Eiden was trying to distract her. He had just moved past Callan, and that's when she found to her relief that Henrik had reached him, ripping the sleeves of Callan's shirt off. One he was tying at the top of his arm, where they both knew the artery was. She assumed the other sleeve would be placed on the wound itself.

"You are a hard nut to break, aren't you?" Eiden swiped his sword in front of her, gaining her attention back.

Joss didn't bother to reply. She didn't want to encourage him.

Eiden charged at her then, sword moving, which she barely blocked at the last minute as she moved backwards. The repeated crashing of steel deafened her ears as she kept moving, almost jogging. Then her foot slipped, and she barely caught herself as she slid to the side. Eiden swiped the sword again, and Joss threw her head back, feeling the air swoosh into her face as the blade missed.

Looking down, she found she had stepped in blood, the body of a knight lying just to the side.

Moving away, she found her grip on the ax again. She was breathing heavily now, the realization that she was almost killed settling in.

"Joss, don't listen to him," Callan was instructing, Henrik still by his side trying to fix his arm. "He's always been full of shit."

"And yet—" Eiden pointed his sword at Joss, making sure he had her full attention "—you know I've been telling the truth."

He was circling the other way now, toying, playing.

Joss followed him, her heart rattling against her ribcage. She tried to calm her breath, but it was the anticipation that was getting to her.

"But in case you don't believe me," Eiden continued, his hand disappearing into his vest. What appeared in his hand next almost caused her to lose the ax.

The bundle of long, golden hair stood out against the blackness of his attire, and as she stared at it, she realized what it was.

Proof of death.

"That could be anyone's," Callan tried to reason as Henrik slowly stood up, calling Joss's name.

She couldn't look at him. All she saw was the hair.

Everyone leaves.

"Joss!" Henrik yelled again as Callan screamed furiously, "He's fucking with you!"

"Am I, though?" Eiden asked, his eyes locking with hers.

It was the doubt, burrowing into her so deep she felt the ache before she realized it was shock forming into a heartbreak.

There was a sudden yell, and immediately Eiden's body jerked, waking Joss from her trance. Eiden was laughing, amused as he held up the knife that was thrown at him, the bundle of hair now on the ground, dropped when he had caught the knife. Stunned, Joss looked at Henrik, finding that he had been the one to throw it.

"Shit," Callan hissed under his breath, the same look crossing Henrik's face, never seeing anyone catch a knife like that before.

"Here, let me show you how it's done properly," Eiden gloated, flipping the knife in his hand so the blade rested in between his fingertips. His gaze took aim on Henrik, his arm pulled back and then he threw it, the knife spiraling into the air—

Clank!

Some screams erupted as the ax collided into the knife, sending it spiraling off to the side. Joss, who had darted forward and thrown the ax in the knife's path, came to a skidding stop as the ax fell to the floor. Quickly picking it up, she faced Eiden, now panting from the exertion.

"Hell, you're a determined little thing," Eiden applauded.

Joss walked by the councilman who was still laying back against one of his comrades, the arrow still buried in his chest. He was paling, his breaths ragged as he remained conscious. "Just hang on," she encouraged as she continued, mimicking the way Eiden circled her. It was his turn to pivot, watching her with a sneer.

"Too bad that determination can't be used in better situations," Eiden was saying, his long strides suddenly coming at her.

Joss held her ground as the sword clashed into the ax. As the sound vibrated into the air, Eiden's foot crashed into her shin, causing her leg to falter, much like he had when she did the same to him. But while she allowed him to recover, Eiden used it to his advantage, his arm suddenly on the handle of the ax. In one quick movement, he jerked it. Not letting go, Joss was pulled forward, allowing him to strike her nose with his forehead. Everything went painfully blurry as her body staggered back, her hand still on the handle.

Eiden threw his boot into her chest to kick her back, but Joss, remembering a move like this before, caught hold of his boot with her other arm. In a tight hold, she twisted, causing Eiden to lose his balance. The surprise was written on his face, not expecting her to have such a firm grip. Automatically, he let go of the ax, and dropping his boot, Joss swung the blade at him, causing Eiden to stagger off to the side.

While Eiden chuckled to himself, Joss quietly thanked the prisoner who helped her learn that move.

"One last chance, Master Brevyn," Eiden coaxed, starting his pacing. "Join me, and I'll pardon you from all this. I'll even make you my personal physician."

"I'm fine where I am," Joss replied, gaining a better grip on her ax. Her nose was bleeding, which she wiped away with the back of her hand. Tears still streamed down her cheeks that she ignored, while the pain in her forehead was making the scene a little fuzzy.

"Oh, stop being so stubborn." Eiden exhaled dramatically. "No one would be fine where you are. Your brother certainly wasn't. Neither was your sister, I hear."

Joss swallowed hard as she gripped the ax, reminding herself to stay focused.

"Being called a witch is a very serious allegation," Eiden continued. "But not as bad as being a coward, like that little brother of yours. I'm sure once you're gone, he'll wish he had stayed. He could have learned from the best." Eiden pointed his sword at her, singling her out. "He would have needed it too, especially since he'll have to pass on the executioner duties to that cute little girl of his. Seems history will repeat itself soon enough."

Nellie, her mind whispered, feeling a chill against the back of her neck.

"Don't listen to him, Joss," Henrik reminded her, remaining by Callan's side.

Eiden laughed. "Oh yes, Joss, don't listen to me. I've only been telling you everything you already know," he mocked.

He was playing with her. She wasn't sure why, but then again, there were a lot of questions she accumulated over her life that she never found answers to. Why a shopkeeper would swindle his family so far into debt he poisoned them all so he wouldn't have to explain what he had done; why a mother would drown her children before going about her day as if nothing had happened; why a serial lover would murder all his mistresses for no reason other than just because he could. There were so many that Joss couldn't even remember them all, but seeing the way Eiden was watching her, he was just like them.

"Leave her alone!" Callan demanded, his voice now yelling behind her. She could hear the tension in it, the pain working its way in.

A laugh escaped, and then Eiden charged her again.

While Joss was able to block the sword with the ax, she wasn't expecting his fist to ram into her side, in the same area Master

Greyson had struck. It awakened the ache that was already there, and she swore she not only felt the crack in her ribs but heard it. Her breath escaped in a gasp. The shrieking sound of metal blazed into her ears as Eiden moved the sword against the ax and then rammed the blade through her leg, causing her to scream.

"No more dancing for the Angel of Death," he gleamed as she fell to the ground, the ax crashing down next to her.

Joss put her hand to the wound, reflexes taking over for an instant, and blood oozed between her fingers as she tried to scoot away. Instantly, she thought of Aric's wound on his thigh, but then Eiden was standing over her, demanding her attention. Reaching for the steel, she recoiled when Eiden went to stomp on her arm, only met with the sound of his boot hitting the floor.

Suddenly, his hands were around her throat, his sword discarded. She pulled at his grip, unable to budge him as she began to choke. She tried hitting at him like she had with Master Greyson, but he widened his arms out, blocking her while keeping his death grip.

This had happened before, the whole reason she was allowed a small pistol in the jailhouse. And just like before, she reached underneath him and grabbed his neck, digging her thumb into the base of his throat. Eiden jerked, the pressure causing him to gag, and his body lifted enough for Joss to ram her knee into his groin. He growled as she let go of his neck and turned so she could ram her elbow into his face. The first hit only stunned him, but the second one caused his teeth to hit her bone. Her entire arm tingled, but she struck him again, his hands faltering from her throat. Eiden raised himself up and threw his fist down, but Joss moved her head, causing him to punch the floor.

The yell bellowed into her face, but she was too busy grabbing his throat again, digging her thumb into the same spot. He tried to tear her hand away, and she struck him along the side of his body with her other fist, feeling the leather withstand her punch. Realizing her error, she was about to aim her fingernails at his eyes when a sudden and clear gunshot split the air.

Both Eiden and Joss froze, staring and hissing at each other. Eiden's dark eyes slowly traveled upward, Joss following his stare by rolling her head back.

Callan was aiming a small pistol in the air—her pistol, which she had forgotten about.

"You know the rules, brother," Eiden panted, though a smile was beginning to show as blood dripped from the corner of his mouth.

"And you know your fight is with me," Callan glared back, the weapon still raised.

Something crossed Eiden's face, and Joss didn't realize it was confusion until she noticed how no arrows were being fired at Callan. That wasn't a part of the plan.

"This is an equal fight," Eiden replied, shifting his weight so it was pinning her more to the ground, hurting her ribcage. "Using a weapon like that will automatically deem you and your pawn here disqualified and sent to the gallows." He looked down at Joss then, adding, "Following in your sister's footsteps, aren't you?"

The pressure of his weight caused her face to redden, and it was already hard to breathe with the crack in her ribs. Rolling her eyes back, she found Callan still kneeling on the floor, the blood caked along the side of his face, the pistol now down. However, she didn't see Henrik.

"But then again, you couldn't use it on me anyway," Eiden continued. "Your honor won't allow it."

"If *you* had learned to have honor, then we'd be done with this game," Callan fired back, and Joss realized he was taunting him. "But I'll give you one last chance."

Eiden chuckled but didn't interrupt.

"Kill me," Callan provoked, lifting his arms up in surrender, the small pistol dropped to the ground. "Let her go, as you said you would, and come claim the crown."

There was a whimper which could only have escaped from Muriel. Everyone else was too quiet, the tension in the room holding them back.

"Oh, really?" Eiden raised an eyebrow. "Because that's not suspicious."

"What the hell am I going to do?" Callan taunted. "Let's end this once and for all."

Eiden lifted himself up, but not before grabbing Joss by the hair and slamming her head back on the ground, putting her in a daze.

Pain warped her mind as she blinked up at him, watching him sit up. He was saying something, wiping the blood from his mouth as his lip curled into a smile, his breaths heavy in satisfaction. And then, just as quickly as stars began to twinkle in her vision, an arm wrapped itself around Eiden's neck, jerking him backwards and leaving her to only see stars against the ceiling.

There were screams, multiple kinds, as something happened at the other end of the room. Although the back of her head was throbbing, Joss rolled over onto her side, lifting herself up onto shaking limbs. Turning her head, she made out through her blurry vision Eiden's dark form striking Henrik, blood already dripping from the lad's temple, below his eye, through his nose, from his lip.

Wobbly and wheezing, Joss lifted herself onto her feet, using the ax as a crutch as she tried to walk towards them, her injured leg slightly dragging from the pain and blood loss. People on either side were yelling for the prince to stop, but no one dared to intervene. An arrow struck the ground off to the side, reminding them of the threat overhead. It was the fear of being next that held them back, which was exactly what the Mask—the prince—had wanted. Despite their best efforts, their voices held no merit to him and became exactly what they were: just noise.

Henrik, her mind was narrowing in, watching as he almost fell into unconsciousness; how his body dropped to the ground, unable to take any more hits. Eiden lifted him up, his hands remaining around his throat as he held him. Henrik tried to cover Eiden's face with his gloved hand, but no one knew it was his cleft hand, while his stronger hand tried to grab at Eiden's fingers. Panic filled his eyes as Eiden kicked his knee, and he fell with Eiden's death lock still around his throat. Despite all the screaming and yelling and begging, she could still hear Henrik's choking gasps as he ran out of air, kneeling before his killer.

They made you into what you are.

The old thief's words whispered to her as she stared at Eiden's back, watching him take the most important thing from her. She dragged herself forward until she stood quietly behind him.

You may die as the town executioner, but what are you really?

She rotated the ax so the blade itself was turned away, leaving the pointed tip at her disposal, aimed and ready.

Figure that out, and don't let anyone take that from you.

Using all the strength she had, Joss swung the ax.

CHAPTER TWENTY-FOUR

Aric heard her voice before he saw her.

"Tie his arm! You must stop the bleeding!"

Thank God, he thought, relief washing over him. If she was able to help, then that meant she was safe; at least, for the moment.

Slinking over to one of the pillars, he was setting his sights on the archer crouched down a couple pillars down. Carefully rounding it, he came to another balcony, his back to the pillar as he surveyed the landscape. He could hear them conversing below, followed by a staccato of clashing steel. Hearing Jocelyn again, he became curious, needing to see her, to make sure she was okay.

Staying low to the ground, he kept to the shadows as he looked beyond the balcony's edge. He could make out two figures fighting in the center of the room, a small group of people huddled underneath the far balcony using it as cover. A few bodies laid dead on the ground, including a woman lying next to a man, the crown just a foot away.

Aric's eyebrow raised a little, not expecting to find the queen dead. His eyes scoured the room, finding Callan on his knees, holding his arm while blood marred the side of his temple and face. Then he recognized Eiden from all those years of seeing glances of him, wielding a sword as he made a wide circle, his focus intent on someone Aric couldn't see, the angle obstructing his view.

Aric smirked at his hunch, wishing he had made a bet with Callan on which brother would betray him.

Then, as Aric pressed forward to see who was holding their ground against Eiden, his curiosity getting the better of him, his gaze fell on the woman... holding the ax....

Shit! His mind screamed, seeing the profile of Jocelyn's face as she pivoted, keeping herself aligned with Eiden. A cold sense of fear drained him as he moved forward, his body reacting before he could stop himself. He saw the way Eiden was eyeing her, noticed the way he handled the sword.

No, not her! He was about to come to his feet until something moved across the way on the other balcony. Catching himself, Aric slunk back into the safety of the shadows. Regaining his composure, he caught sight of another hooded figure before it disappeared into the darkness.

Snapping awake, Aric took one last look below before moving back to his original position against the pillar, his back to the marble. With the knife in hand, he was eyeing past the next pillar, trying to catch sight of the archer he was stalking and telling himself to focus. He couldn't help her if he was killed.

"I hear Aric Kayden was a hard man to impress, and yet, you managed it."

Aric's anxiousness vibrated under his skin, recognizing that voice. He had heard it so many times in his nightmare, the Mask who tortured and tormented him. But then he remembered the body in Traitor's Alley, and looking in their direction, he became hesitant. He knew that tone; knew nothing good ever came from it.

"The way he was with those harlots—" a whistle drew out then "—I'm a little surprised he even considered you."

There was no reason for his jaw to clench the way it did, given that it wasn't a far-off statement. He had had his fun; lots of it. Even if things with Andrina were destined to end abruptly anyway, the old him would have found another harlot to take her place; that's just how it was. But with Jocelyn, there was no one else. And having to hear her listen to those things made his nerves crawl, like being outed in front of a crowd. He wasn't ashamed of his past, and yet, his gut turned just the same. Her opinion of him meant more than he realized.

It was when he heard Callan come to the defense, reminding Jocelyn—and Aric—that his brother wasn't someone to trust that Aric fell back into focusing on the task at hand. He was making his way to the other pillar, knife poised, when he heard Henrik and Callan yelling, driving his attention back to them.

In the light, he saw the bundle of blonde hair in Eiden's grip. He watched the plan unfold, and even in the distance between them, he watched as it affected her. Jocelyn's stance hadn't changed, yet something had—the way she hesitated, the way she was breathing hard. He almost leapt up onto the balcony to prove the man wrong until movements across the way grabbed his attention, reminding him of what he needed to do.

Kill them all, his mind ordered.

The archer didn't have a chance to fully lift his bow when Aric rounded the pillar, taking the man on in just a couple of strides. Pushing the hooded figure up against the pillar, he had the blade hilt deep into the man's throat, right below the mask he wore. The gargling was hushed behind the mask, no one around hearing as the body convulsed before slowly dying off. Aric lowered the body to the ground, and yanking the blade out, placed it dripping back in his boot, knowing he'd have to clean it later.

Staying bent down on one knee, he unhooked the quiver and slipped it from the body. Buckling it in place against his back, the leather strap was snug against his chest as it ran diagonally from shoulder to hip. Picking the bow and a loose arrow off the floor, he heard a *clank* before a couple of screams erupted. Peeking over the balcony's edge, he found Jocelyn was still on her feet, picking her ax up while Eiden stalked her.

"Hell, you're a determined little thing," the younger prince was applauding. Aric's nerves ached in wanting to cut the man's throat.

Just keep it up a little longer, sweetheart, Aric thought, taking one more look at Jocelyn, remembering his promise to her.

Hearing something shuffle down the way, he put an arrow in place and rotated around, keeping behind the pillar. Arrow drawn, he inched out, met with an arrow striking the pillar right in front of him. A dark form shifted in the shadows, causing him to release his arrow. It scraped against his hand holding the bow, followed by a brief pause before a hissing grunt echoed in return, hitting its target.

Drawing another arrow from the quiver and notching it to the bow string, he rounded the pillar and made it to the next balcony. Staying down, he peered again, finding two dark movements instead of one. Someone had come to their comrade's aide.

Pulling a second arrow, he turned his bow slightly sideways, positioning one arrow against the other. Inching out again, he caught the two dark figures already coming closer. He was fluid in how he pulled the string back and then let go, releasing the arrows. One hit its mark, causing the body to drop. The other hit someone in the side, who slunk back out of sight.

Aric was rounding the pillar when something sliced his own side. He ducked behind the pillar, realizing an arrow had grazed him. Given all he had endured so far, the wound itself was more of an annoyance, just deep enough to bleed.

He could hear Eiden's voice again but tuned it out, trying to listen for something else. Then he heard it: the quick succession of footsteps.

Pulling another arrow, he quietly sat the bow down and faced the pillar. As the hooded figure rounded the corner, his own bow and arrow in position, Aric was able to elbow the man in the arm, the bow flinging sideways, sending the arrow off into the distance without a target. The mask faced him, and Aric used his surprise to his advantage, gripping the man by the throat as he plunged his arrowhead in the man's eye. He tried to scream, but with Aric's hand around his throat and the mask already muffling his voice, the sound went unnoticed to those below.

Knowing he was still alive, Aric pulled the arrow out and stabbed it into the eye again, trying to hit the kill spot. Suddenly, the man jolted, and Aric caught sight of a figure down the way taking aim with his bow, striking his comrade in the back. Aric pushed the body forward, using him as a shield as the archer at the end released another arrow, hitting the body in the leg and causing him to slip a little from Aric's grasp.

And then the gunshot was fired.

Everyone scattered, the figure at the end bolting towards the closest balcony as Aric dropped the body he was carrying and kept his cover behind a pillar. Using the reprieve, Aric hurried back to where he dropped the bow, picking it up as he stayed down on one knee. Looking at the scene below, he found the shot had come from Callan. Then he saw Jocelyn being pinned down by Eiden, and something in him snapped.

His hand pulled the arrow out from the quiver, already having it positioned in place before he realized what he was doing. Taking aim in between the railing, he was about to release the arrow when he noticed someone coming up behind Eiden, keeping quiet under the cover of those who never gave away he was there.

Henrik! Aric wanted to call out to him, to tell him he had a better angle, he'd kill this man for them like he was supposed to. But this was Henrik, loyal to the end, even when he didn't stand a chance against his opponent.

"Kill me." Callan dropped the small gun, lifting his arms up. Knowing the prince, he already caught on that it was an act. "Let her go, as you said you would, and come claim the crown."

Taking the scene in, Aric knew Callan was only keeping Eiden distracted. The younger prince obviously didn't believe it, but the curiosity was getting the better of him.

Callan, however, kept the antics up. "Let's end this once and for all."

It was when Eiden grabbed Jocelyn by the hair and struck her head against the hard ground that he wanted so badly to beat Henrik to the punch. But then the lad had his arm around the prince, dragging him off Jocelyn. He had a good hold too, until Eiden threw his head back, striking Henrik right in the face. The lad was dazed, and effortlessly, Eiden turned the tables on him, one hand holding the lad by the collar while his fist rammed repeatedly into him. Henrik tried his best to cover his head, being pushed farther back with each strike.

The room became alive then, everyone yelling for Eiden to let the lad go. Callan was one thing, Jocelyn even a worthy opponent, but not Henrik. He didn't even have a weapon.

It was like being back in the forest and watching those three would-be bounty hunters attack him for fun. It had been hard to watch, but not like this, knowing Eiden's capabilities. Aric's own scars itched with anticipation, remembering his cruelty.

He had just taken aim again, about to release the arrow straight into Eiden's back, when someone kicked the side of his face. The arrow shot through the railing and off to the ground below, causing shrieks to erupt as people thought the arrow was a warning for them. The boot swung at him again, and Aric blocked the attack by grabbing it and then lifting his leg and ramming his own boot into the attacker's knee. A *crack* sounded off as the body fell sideways, crashing into the pillar.

Aric rolled himself over, coming to his feet in one quick movement. The attacker pivoted away when Aric's arm caught him around the throat. His assailant pushed against his body, trying to throw his head back, but Aric had already watched his leader pull the same tactic. Turning his head out of the way, his back hit the pillar as he tightened his arm, the hooded man trying to grab at him but unable to unhook his hold.

Aric was just settling into the headlock, the man unable to stop him, when he heard the yells below turn into horrified gasps as a single scream pierced the air.

He turned in time to see Jocelyn swing her ax, striking the pointed part right into Eiden's side. The point punctured him, and Eiden screamed as he fell sideways, landing on his knees. Henrik fell back onto the ground, covered in his own blood.

Jocelyn hobbled towards him, using the ax as a cane before taking it back up into her hands and swung, striking Eiden again in the side. Another scream pierced the room, gasps from their audience trailing afterwards, as he rolled over onto the floor. He began crawling, the group around him parting desperately to get away from him. Jocelyn was trying to trail after him, dragging her leg with her ax in her hands, when suddenly Eiden caught hold of something. Coming unsteadily to his feet, he held it in his hands, causing Jocelyn to come to a quick halt.

Even in the distance, Aric could see it was a knife. He would have almost lost his grip on the body if it wasn't for the dark form emerging from around the side. Aric rotated just in time for an arrow to sink into the man he was holding, the force hitting Aric against the pillar.

Picking the man up from under his arms, Aric moved forward, feeling another arrow hit the body before ramming it against the other assailant, knocking him to the ground. Something came around his neck, and suddenly Aric found himself in a headlock, surprised by the assailant he hadn't seen there.

You promised her, his mind flashed, and while losing air was making him panic, he lifted his leg, pulling the knife out of his boot. Pushing back against his attacker, he swung his arm out and then behind him, sinking the knife into the man's side. A muffled shriek erupted, the arms slipping from Aric's neck, who slammed his body back against the man, knocking him onto the ground.

The dark form in front of him had pushed his comrade off and bolted, and if Aric had been quick enough, he would have been able to meet him on the stairs and kill him. But then he heard someone scream, someone who sounded an awful lot like Henrik. There were others too, but that one scream rocked against him, putting him on alert.

Running back to the pillar, he looked out past the railing. Eiden was moving to the center of the room, Jocelyn a few paces away. While she was bent over a little, she was still standing. At first, he was relieved, until he found she was trembling, the hilt of the knife sticking out from her shoulder.

Kill them all.

The thought came to him in more than just a feeling; it was a purpose. He grabbed the bow he dropped and moved, passing each balcony under the cover of darkness, searching for the right angle. The noises below fell silent on him; his mind was buzzing too much in its own rage. If any other masked figures were around, they had already fled, leaving him alone up there on the second floor. He knew they wouldn't get far, though. He'd hunt them all down. He had to, for her.

But first, he'd take down the most important one: the one who had hired him. Finding an angle he could work with, Aric took his position, and looked past the point of the arrow at his mark.

Because this was his job, the whole reason he was there. And he was going to happily do it for free.

CHAPTER TWENTY-FIVE

Joss had only closed her eyes for a moment, but she swore she could see him on the side of the road, bruised and bleeding in the undergrowth. She saw the way the leaves moved in the sunlight, matching the color of one of his eyes. She still felt the empathy she had for him, as if feeling his pain.

But then something woke her from her daze, and it was when her eyes reopened that the pain enveloped her, becoming real and reminding her that the wounds were all hers. She tried moving out of the way when she caught sight of Henrik's knife in Eiden's hand, but her injured leg faltered, helping the blade to catch her in the right shoulder. The momentum had pushed her back a couple steps, but somehow, she had remained on her feet.

It was almost poetic how her wounds matched Aric's. The only difference was he had been found and saved. She, on the other hand, had lost.

"At least you were a worthy opponent," Eiden was smiling, moving awkwardly over to where his dead brother laid.

The ax had done its job, penetrating through the leather vest and puncturing him. She wasn't quite sure how deadly the blows had been, given that Eiden was still trudging around. He was stiff, injured, but still very much alive.

Grunting as he bent down, Eiden caught hold of the crown, placing it on his head. "But everything has to come to an end," he continued, and turning, he moved towards her.

Joss wheezed as she backed away from him, using the ax as support. Every movement seemed to pull against the blade rammed into her shoulder, and she groaned through clenched teeth as Eiden stalked after her at a slow pace.

"No! Fight *me*!" Henrik was screaming through gasps. A couple of the men snuck to his aide, holding him back as he tried to stand up.

"Eiden!" Callan called out, and Joss heard him rising awkwardly to his feet behind her. "This is our fight! No one else needs to be involved."

"When all the time passes and all these people are gone," Eiden started in, staring right at Joss, his tone calmer than it should have been.

"Eiden!" Callan yelled again as Henrik struggled against the men who held him back.

"Even when all the wars rage and all the kings fall," Eiden continued, ignoring them as he picked up the sword he had dropped. He staggered a bit in doing so, but then it was in his hand, ready. Joss hadn't realized she had passed by it.

Seeing the threat, Joss came to a stop, knowing she couldn't outrun him. Bringing a hand to the knife, she felt the worn handle, knowing it well from all the times Henrik practiced with it; from all the times her father used it before giving it to him. With a couple aching breaths, she yanked the blade out, which slipped from her hand and fell to the floor as the pain sharpened its hold on her, making her scream through her teeth. She knew she was running out of time now; the blood loss from her leg alone was making her lightheaded, and the wound to her shoulder would only make things more fatal if she didn't get the bleeding under control. She had learned from past experiences, from finding others in these same predicaments.

"You'll still be a deathsman," Eiden concluded, smiling a little at the bloody mess he had created. "*That's* the answer to the old man's question."

"Joss, get away from him!" Callan ordered, but his voice was airy in her mind, just another far-off plea.

Joss gripped the handle of the ax, her fingers numb. She tried to plant her feet like she would on the gallows, right at the block. Lifting the ax into both hands, she embraced the familiar way it handled. Despite the stance, her muscles shook, one arm now weaker than the other, and her lungs continued to wheeze with each labored breath.

"Please!" Henrik called out again, struggling, begging. "She's all I have!"

Joss looked at her old friend, the last brother that she had. She wanted to tell him it was okay, but all that came out was a grunt, the pain stealing her words.

"I'm doing you a favor," Eiden was saying, blocking Joss's view of Henrik as he came to a stop a little ways from her. "I'll make sure his death is less painful."

Joss stood there staring at him, her breaths labored from the cracked ribs, her body trembling from the spasms running across her shoulder and leg. She'd deal at least one final blow; that's what she told herself. He'd live past her, but he wouldn't live unscathed. The ax would make sure of it.

And, if fate were kind, maybe Callan would have his chance.

"Say hello to your assassin for me," Eiden smiled, the sword sturdy in hand.

He barely took a step toward her when something struck him from behind. He jerked a little, wincing but unmarked. Eiden turned around, and that's when Joss saw an arrow sticking out of his back, stuck in the leather vest.

Joss's eyes went to Henrik, finding him and the others just as surprised by the attack. Her gaze then rose to the balcony, seeing a hooded shadow against the railing.

"The hell—" Eiden was shouting before another arrow was fired, hitting him right in the leg. A frustrated yell struck the air as suddenly another arrow landed, hitting him on the other leg. Eiden growled, falling to his knees as the pain forced his legs to give out.

Joss's gaze fell to the glittering crown, and then to Eiden, yelling and cursing from where he was kneeling.

She had seen that stance before: the kneeling convict, the executioner waiting behind with the sword. All those years of watching rushed towards her, all the times she watched others beheaded with a sword but never being allowed the chance.

You have to strike sideways. Quinn's words came to her then as she dragged herself forward, the ax waiting in hand. *That takes a lot of strength.*

It had been a subtle criticism, alluding to the fact that she was a woman in a man's role. But as she stood behind Eiden, eyeing his neck—the width and length, things she always took into consideration—she ignored that part. Eiden was right; she was still a deathsman.

Joss allowed her body to move in memory: taking her stance, gripping the ax just right. She kept her eye on the spot on his neck as she retracted the ax, this time being sideways instead of up. The pain in her shoulder protested but she growled through it.

Eiden was turning his head to look back at her, a glimpse of his sneer evident, when she swung. She put everything into that swing—the pain, the heartbreak, the desperation. And as the blade struck his neck, she didn't realize it had cleanly gone through until she staggered to the side from her own momentum and Eiden's head and crown fell to the floor. His body collapsed forward, separated.

Wheezing harder, her body tightening from the exertion, Joss looked over, seeing what she had done. Taking in the decapitation, her eyes immediately went to the spot on the balcony, finding the dark shadow was gone.

No one in the room moved. There weren't jeers or hoots like from past executions. There weren't even gasps. Just silence and her own breathing.

Seeing the crown, Joss limped over to it. Pressing the blade of the ax to the floor, she leaned against the handle as she bent down and picked it up. Looking at it, she marveled a little at the gold and jewels.

What are you really? Charleston Ore's question came to mind.

Pivoting around, Joss found Callan standing where he had been on the floor, his dark eyes round in disbelief that matched others in the room. Blood seeped through the bandage on his arm, which he still held with his hand.

Joss limped a couple steps towards him before her injured leg gave out, causing her to stop. She leaned against the ax handle, the pain overwhelming her to the point she had to squeeze her eyes shut, tears coming to her aide. Opening her eyes, she found Callan was limping slowly towards her, the shock in his dark face deepening into something soft, unlike the hard persona she spent days traveling with.

She held onto the handle of the ax as she lifted the crown up for Callan to take. Because that was the answer to the old thief's question: She helped. She always helped—saving a lost prince from the gallows, making sure deaths were merciful, finding people on the side of the road and bringing them home so she could treat their wounds.

The gallows had never defined her. Her heart did.

Callan's eyes went to the crown, but as he continued forward, he didn't take it. Instead, he pushed it out of his way as he went straight to her, his arms suddenly around her in a tight embrace. Confused, Joss asked, "But the crown..."

"Fuck the crown," he whispered into her shoulder, seeing what power had done to his own family.

Joss returned the hug with her one good arm, and when Callan finally pulled away, she found it was because Henrik had approached. His bruised and bloody face looked at her with relief, tears sparkling in his eyes that he didn't bother hiding.

"You okay?" he whispered, a tear falling.

Before she could reply, Callan pulled him to his side, bringing the three into a tight embrace. It had been the three of them all those days, and even now it was just them, relishing all they had gone through together; each of them torn and bleeding in their own ways but all for the same purpose.

"You're family now, you know," Callan told them, and Joss and Henrik really couldn't object, only nod.

Callan was the first to hear someone else approaching, and as he turned, he found it was Muriel.

"You're home," she whispered, her own tears showing, timid in how to approach them.

It only took Callan a few long, limping strides to reach her, his mouth already on hers, his arms holding her tight to his chest, which she sank into. It didn't matter his clothes were dirty or covered in blood from his own wounds. Neither broke apart from that kiss, feeding on years of waiting. When the group of councilmen and ladies began to come out from hiding, some even coming to interrupt their reunion to welcome Callan home, he never let Muriel go.

Unable to stand anymore, Henrik helped Joss lie down on the floor, sitting with her as he took his shirt off and pressed it to her shoulder wound.

"You don't have to do that," she whispered, seeing the blood still fresh on his face, the skin welting and turning deep purple in places.

"You didn't have to fight him," Henrik reminded her, his

words a little off given his swollen lip.

"You didn't either," she wheezed back, making both smile, knowing they would have made the same choices if given a second chance.

A few of the councilmen approached, finding the state she was in. Offering to help, they took off their cloaks, one rolling it up to put it under her head for support, the other pressing it against the wound in her leg.

"That was an astonishing hit," one was marveling at her as he undid his belt to secure it around the upper part of her leg. Once in place, he tightened it to help stop the bleeding.

"It comes with the job," she tried to joke, and he seemed to smile at her from underneath his beard and mustache. He continued to apply pressure to her leg with his cloak. "Good thing it does," he agreed, winking at her before he turned to acknowledge Henrik, admiring how hard he had fought.

Despite the attention, Joss still held onto the crown, everyone seeming to forget it, or at least thinking it was in good enough hands for what had transpired. As she looked over at Callan and Muriel, his wounds being treated by the ladies, she could see how the two looked at each other—quick glances, soft smiles. Joss grinned at their reunion until she caught sight of the golden hair lying on the floor in the distance. Her smile faltered a little, remembering the arrows that had struck Eiden. Then, she turned her head to look up at the balcony where she had seen the hooded figure standing.

Even with the interrupting noises occurring on the other side of the massive doors, she looked for him.

Even when they were all finally rescued, the doors pulled open and revealing the battle it took for the knights to get in, she still wondered if he would come back, like he had promised.

CHAPTER TWENTY-SIX

Per Callan's orders, they had all been bed-ridden.

Joss knew it was for their healing, and the way the physicians were coming and going, all had been stitched up and on the mend. The thymelock salve they used—undiluted, unlike hers at home—helped shorten their healing time, but as the second and third week passed by, Callan still insisted they stay. "For me, for just a little longer," he had told them, and they found that when he had said they were family, he meant it. Besides Muriel, they were all he had left of his former life.

There were no signs of Aric.

The masked figures who barricaded the doors, the knights explained, had only been breached by the arrows that suddenly struck them, helping the knights to get ahold of the situation. It had been a battle, some lives lost, but in the end, it was the mysterious archer who helped them win the day.

"See, he's not dead," Henrik spoke up one night, after the maids left and the physicians had done their rounds.

Callan had put them in a very elegant room with two beds situated on either side. By the placement of the furniture, Joss realized the second bed had been brought in just for them so they could stay together. On one side of the room, large glass double doors overlooked a garden while on the other side was a glowing fire crackling in a marble hearth. Joss laid back against the large, plush pillows and stared across the way at Henrik. While their clothes were discarded, they had been left with silk-made attire that felt good to be in, especially after spending so many days in the same dirty clothes. Washed and cleaned, the two were enjoying their time—Joss, who watched her own healing progress, and Henrik, who feasted on the food.

"I'd bet money he's gone off to track down more of those masked goons and rid this place of them." Henrik popped a grape in his mouth, hoarding his own bowl that was placed on a table near him.

It wasn't a far-fetched idea. Aric had even tried killing her just to get his job done.

Joss nodded in response as the far door near the fireplace opened and Callan walked in right on time. Every morning and every night, even while healing from his own wounds, he checked on them, often sharing meals or going for walks so he and Joss could regain their mobility. The thymelock had worked well on him too; his own limping was gone, his arm fully functional again. He gave them tours of the castle, walked the battlements at night, per Joss's request, so she could see the castle in torchlight. There was so much to be done—council meetings, funeral preparations—and yet, Callan always came to see them. Muriel was usually with him, appearing before him if he was running late, but this time she was absent.

"Letting her sleep, eh?" Henrik winked at him, clearly feeling better.

"I don't understand why she puts up with you," Callan replied, nodding to Joss. In his smile, though, they knew he was teasing. He was also dressed in all black, a continuous sign that the realm was still in mourning for the royal family.

"I'm a delight," Henrik rebutted.

"You're still medicated," Joss pointed out. The physicians had given them both some strong dosages to help with the aftereffects of their wounds. Joss knew the ingredients, understanding the best way to wean someone off was by slowly decreasing the dosages instead of taking them off completely. It was another reason Callan told them to stay, despite Joss knowing how to make the concoction and could have weaned them off herself.

"I can't help it," Henrik replied, popping another grape into his mouth.

"I can. I'll have the physicians wean you off quicker," Callan teased, settling into a chair he put in front of the double doors. He sat between the two beds so he could address his guests.

"I know you both will want to go home soon," he admitted. "I've had new clothes tailored for you based on the clothes you were wearing, and your ax and knife have been cleaned. And I've already sent both criers and messengers to Galmoor, letting them know what you've done for the crown. You'll be given a generous stipend, which I'll make sure is passed down to your children and grandchildren."

Joss sat up a little. "You really don't have to—"

"I do," Callan interrupted her. "You two have done so much for me, and like I said, you're family now. I take care of my family." He looked at her knowingly, then. "I've also sent that favor you asked for—for your friend."

The words even sobered Henrik, and they both whispered a "thank you" to the new king.

"When do you think you'll leave?" Callan asked, looking from Henrik to Joss.

"We should probably start heading back by the end of the week," Joss admitted, knowing that's when their final dosages would be given.

Her cracked ribs were long healed, and even the wounds to her leg and shoulder had healed tremendously in their own right, the stitches removed barely a day ago thanks to the thymelock. Her mobility was still stiff, but with time she knew she'd get it back.

"I'll have everything ready for you, then." Callan stood up. "I unfortunately have an early morning meeting to attend, but I'll visit afterwards."

"Of course," Joss smiled, thanking him again, which he smiled in return as he made his way to the door.

"And just so you know," Callan added, turning back to face them. "You're always welcome here. Anytime. And if you need anything at all, send me a crier. It doesn't matter if it's in a week, a year, twenty years—I will always be at your service."

The two nodded, thanking him again, and he turned away, leaving the room with the door closing quietly behind him.

While both Joss and Henrik were beyond grateful for his

kindness, the two looked at each other, disheartened, the same thought crossing their minds.

He had never mentioned a pardon.

When the day came to leave, Joss and Henrik were in their room, dressed and ready. Callan had their attire match what they previously wore in color and size, though the quality was much finer. The physicians and maids had said their goodbyes to them, and as Joss was putting her small pistol in her new boot—given back to her from Callan the night before—the door quietly opened.

Muriel entered, her elegant black gown and diamonds making her the queen they had always imagined. While Joss and Henrik bowed, she immediately approached, pulling Joss up into a hug. "None of that, you two," she reminded them as she smiled at Joss before going to hug Henrik. "I wanted to come here and personally thank you again, for everything."

She took each of their hands now, squeezing them in unison.

"Now, your horses are saddled and ready," she continued, getting down to business, "and we're sending a wagon with extra food and supplies, along with your ax and knife. A handful of knights will travel with you to make sure you get home safely."

"Thank you, but we'll honestly be fine, Your Majesty," Joss insisted, not used to all the attention.

"*Muriel,*" she corrected her. "Also, Callan is stuck in another meeting, but he wants to say his goodbyes. He would like for you to meet him in the Meeting Hall, which I'm here to take you to."

Joss and Henrik didn't think much of it as they followed Muriel out, finding a couple of knights waiting to escort them. The group headed down the halls, Joss and Henrik feeling lost in all the finery. Despite their walks and tours with Callan, it was all still overwhelming, the beauty overpowering them each time they stepped out into the hallway.

As they came to the entrance of the meeting hall, however, both Joss and Henrik came to a quiet halt at the scene before them.

The public chamber sunk down, candelabras buzzing with electricity which lit the room while rows of benches rose from the circular floor. At the head of the room, chairs sat in a half- circle, the councilmen standing behind them, looking their way. Callan stood at the head, his hands locked in front of him, a warrior at rest. However, it was on those benched rows that sat a multitude of people, every space filled with an onlooker who now turned to stare at them.

Caught off guard but wanting to stay in step with Muriel, the two made their way down the staircase, passing the murmurs and stares. The two knights who had escorted them, however, remained at the entrance.

"What's going on?" Henrik whispered. Joss shook her head, equally confused.

Reaching the ground floor, they were led to the center of the circle, only stopping when Callan gently put his hand up. Muriel had continued on, coming to sit on a throne-like chair behind Callan, placed there just for her. On the other side of her was a clerk sitting at a small desk keeping records like they did in Galmoor during trials and proceedings.

Swallowing hard, Joss and Henrik remained standing close to each other, Henrik looking around at the people who were whispering amongst themselves while the councilmen took their seats. Joss, however, could only look from Muriel to Callan, reading their faces, which gave nothing away.

"Master Jocelyn Brevyn, Town Executioner of Galmoor," Callan announced, hushing the crowd. "And Mr. Henrik Vanzant, the Executioner's Assistant."

Henrik faced forward with her, both staring at the man who looked at them with a small but formal grin.

"I have a confession to make, which is hard to say, given how much you've done for me and this realm," Callan continued. "But my late brother, Eiden Ronen, was right about me. Despite all we've been through together, I wasn't going to pardon you."

The words felt like a pinprick, and Joss had to blink away the disappointment lying dormant in her chest, waiting for this moment.

"It wasn't out of malice or tradition or even laziness, on the part of the crown or myself. It was because of you two; what you do for people." Callan laid his gaze on Joss. "There is no hiding the fact that you're a woman who had to take on a male role, forcing you to take lives; and yet, despite the brutality, you kept your morale, your professionalism, and your compassion. You remained human in a very inhumane profession. You are the embodiment of mercy, especially for those who need it most, both in death and all those you've helped heal throughout your years.

"And you, Henrik." Callan now turned to the lad. "You've stood by her side through it all; as an assistant, as a brother. You take equal part in it, including the loyalty you have for her."

Henrik shifted, uncomfortable that he was being singled out

but knowing it was true.

"But I know my decision to not pardon you isn't fair to you both. I've seen what this job has done to you and your family. So, council," Callan lifted his arms, addressing the men sitting in the chairs. "I place this before you, as peers who not only want the best for their kingdom, but who have seen firsthand the heroism of these two during our darkest moment. 'Agree' will pardon Master Brevyn and Mr. Vanzant from the duties of being executioner; 'deny' will keep things as they are. Majority rules." Callan's eyes then rested on Joss and Henrik. "And no matter the outcome, you and your family will be taken care of by this realm for as long as my bloodline holds the throne."

A quiet pause drew out before Callan announced to the council, "The decision is bestowed upon you."

Henrik shifted again, but Joss couldn't look his way. Hope was edging in, and she didn't want to act on it in case the council decided with Callan. *At least he was honest*, she reminded herself, not wanting to hate him, though feeling the effects of knowing that all those years hoping for a pardon had been wasted. It twisted her gut in how hopeful her father had been during each letter, begging to be free, when it had never been an option.

Murmuring swept through the room but died off as the first councilman stood from his chair.

Joss had just bowed her head, wishing she wasn't there, when she heard it.

"Agree."

Joss blinked, staring at the ground. *What?*

The next one stood up. "Agree."

Joss turned her head, finding the councilman who had held his cloak against the wound on her leg. He bowed his head at her, grinning.

She would have smiled back, but the next councilman who stood made her gasp a little.

"Agree."

Joss looked at Callan, seeing he was trying to hide his grin. Muriel remained seated behind him, a hand to her lips, trying to hide the quivering of her own smile that was being brought on by tears.

"Agree."

Joss's own eyes became blurry as she turned to Henrik. He didn't look at her at first, his head back, his eyes squeezed shut, the emotions washing over him as he relished in the words he was hearing.

"Agree."

When he finally brought his head down, eyes opening, he met her gaze. It was the same face he made when he was little, standing on the gallows when she took the noose off from around his neck.

"Agree."

Save him. She never told anyone, even Henrik, that she had said those words to her father; that it was at her request he asked for Henrik's pardon, taking the orphan under his care. No one else would claim him, except her.

"Agree."

She smiled up at Henrik then, the same smile she gave to him as a child. While her siblings had stood off in the crowd, Joss was the one who was called to take the noose off. She had led Henrik down the steps and stood next to him, hand in hand, as they watched the execution proceed without him. It had been her because she was the one who had asked.

"Agree."

It was Joss who now reached for Henrik's hand, much like she did the day they met. Though his hand was larger now, there was still that same grip, the same surprising strength in his cleft hand. She watched him take a deep breath, the emotions written on his face but unable to put them into words.

"Agree."

"Majority rule," she whispered, realizing they had long passed the halfway mark. Without warning, Henrik pulled her into his chest, his head bowed next to hers as he held onto her tightly. "Your father was proud of you. I told him to tell you. I should have said something when he didn't," his whisper came out.

"Agree."

Joss held onto him. "I told him to save you," she whispered into his shoulder. She never thought to tell him, only because saving him from the gallows meant she had damned him to an executioner's life. She was the reason he couldn't have the woman he loved; why everyone truly looked at him differently, like an outcast, like her.

"Agree."

Henrik moved his head a little, and she swore she could feel his lop-sided grin next to her ear. "I know," he replied simply, the whole reason he always stayed by her side.

"Agree."

The tears were falling down her cheeks as she hung onto Henrik. Both knew it was over, but they still hung onto each other, like they always had, all while a lifetime of darkness lifted in a single moment. But as they stood there, someone else spoke out; someone they weren't expecting.

"Agree!"

Pulling away, the two looked up at the single man standing among the crowd. They didn't know him or even recognize him, but there he was, agreeing. A woman stood up next to him, yelling out, "Agree!"

Another in the corner stood up, and then another towards the back. A couple in the front stood, and then, slowly, one by one, each person in the room came to their feet, the chorus of "Agrees" filling the air.

Joss stared in wonderment as the scene unfolded before them, the "Agrees" taking over the proceeding. As she turned back to look at Callan, she instead caught sight of Muriel standing from her chair, yelling "Agree" as tears streaked her face.

When her gaze finally fell on Callan, she was met with a knowing smile. "Agree," he whispered, against the shouting and applause that erupted, confirming that the woman deathsman and her assistant—and the Brevyn bloodline—had finally been pardoned.

CHAPTER TWENTY-SEVEN

"The pardon came in a couple weeks ago."

Joss stared at Lord Hilcox as he peered back down at the parchment. She hadn't seen the old councilman since the day Callan stood trial in that very room. While she and Henrik had only returned home scarcely two hours ago, word spreading throughout the town of their arrival, they had already been summoned to Judgment Hall. It didn't help that they had arrived with the king's knights, the gold and burgundy banners giving them away.

Callan never revealed that he had already pardoned them, dispatched with the messengers he'd sent out. She tried not to grin when she remembered seeing his knowing smile among the applause and "agrees."

"And Lord Wolburn?" she asked, picturing the councilman who had betrayed them. The last time she saw him, he had run off, yelling for the guards after she helped save Callan from his own hanging.

"Let's just say," Lord Hilcox smiled, eyeing her, "we've cleaned house while you were gone. Per our new king's orders."

Joss nodded, accepting the answer, though she did wonder what punishment Callan would think up for the councilman who tried to have him executed.

As she and Henrik both stood waiting in front of the risen pulpit that Lord Hilcox sat behind, Joss looked about the room, finding things hadn't changed. The courtroom was still as spacious and well-lit as she remembered, smelling of polished wood. The chandelier overhead and candelabras against the wall were all well-lit, even though only one councilman was in attendance. Overall, the room was empty, leaving Joss and Henrik—as well as the clerk dictating the proceeding sitting off to the side—as the only ones in attendance, before the far door opened, and Quinn entered the room.

Upon seeing them, the head jailer faltered in step but quickly regained himself, the surprise evident on his face.

"Master Terrif, we've been waiting for you," Lord Hilcox greeted as Quinn took his place next to Joss, Henrik standing just on the other side.

"Sorry, sir," he greeted, eyeing Joss and Henrik with a grin that was barely seen underneath his beard.

"As you've heard, we have a little bit of a situation," Lord Hilcox explained, folding his hands on top of the table. "The king has pardoned Master Brevyn and Mr. Vanzant, relieving them of their duties. Have the criers been sent out?"

"Yes, sir," Quinn noted. "I'm sure an executioner in one of the neighboring towns would be more than happy to put us on their roster."

It was a lie, but for the right price they'd eventually find someone.

"I hear Burnlyn is having the same issues since their deathsman mysteriously vanished." Lord Hilcox looked them over, seeing if they had heard the news.

Master Greyson. Joss and Henrik said nothing, knowing his mutilated corpse was rotten or eaten beyond recognition by now.

"We'll find someone," Quinn reassured him.

"Yes, yes," Lord Hilcox replied, already scanning over the parchment again. "There's also the matter of the new head jailer."

That's when Quinn faltered. "New jailer?" he asked.

"Why, yes," Lord Hilcox smiled. "I have here a parchment written by his Royal Majesty, Callan Ronen, who hereby pardons Master Quinn Terrif of his duties as Head Jailer of Galmoor."

Quinn's mouth opened and then quickly shut, turning to stare at Joss and Henrik.

Joss tried to act nonchalant but had a poor time of hiding her smile. "You helped him too," she whispered, not giving away it was the favor she asked Callan for. While she wasn't sure if a pardon for the jailer was possible, she did ask that he receive some financial security for the trouble he went through in helping them escape. Maybe allow him to retire earlier than planned. Callan, however, had a better idea.

Quinn blinked at her, and as reality sunk in, so did the little grin. With his eyes misting over, he batted the emotion away, trying to remain as the firm jailer.

"So, with that said, I hereby confirm that Master Quinn Terrif is free of his duties as Head Jailer and given a full stipend for his services." Smiling, he added, "It was a pleasure working with you, sir."

Quinn nodded profusely, unable to speak, knowing the emotions would come out instead of words.

"As for you two," Lord Hilcox said, turning to Joss and Henrik, "it was always a pleasure working with you both as well. I wish you all the best of luck on your next endeavors, Mr. Vanzant and—" he smiled at Joss "—*Miss* Brevyn."

"Thank you, sir," both Joss and Henrik replied. Being directed out of the room, the three made their way out of Judgment Hall, passing the familiar hallways, nodding to familiar guards. Once on the street, however, they shed their formalities and were embraced heartily by a very emotional Quinn, who was never one to give hugs or let his feelings show.

"We're free," he was murmuring to a very stunned Henrik after he gripped him in a tight hug. Wiping his eyes, Quinn placed his hands on his hips, taking in a deep breath of the fresh air. "I can't wait to see my wife's face," he chuckled.

"So, what are you going to do with yourself now?" Henrik asked as they stood in the sunlight, Judgment Hall a mere shadow behind them.

"I have no idea," Quinn admitted. "But I can't wait to find out."

Joss grinned as a cart passed by, greeting them. "Good day, sirs," the man greeted before turning to Joss. "Good day, Miss."

Joss smiled and bowed her head, stunned he had acknowledged her. News had circulated of what they had done for Aselian, thanks to Callan's messengers and criers. Each town they arrived in, already attracted to the wagon and knights, welcomed them with open arms, giving them the best lodgings and ample amounts of food and drink. But being home was different. No one here had ever paid much attention to her or Henrik, at least not in a positive way. Seeing how things were changing felt a little strange.

"Not used to it yet, are you?" Quinn winked at her.

Joss shrugged as she admitted, "It'll take some getting used to."

She was overlooking the square until she realized Quinn was eyeing her. "What?" she asked, seeing he was curious about something; even a little suspicious.

"Did you really behead him while he was kneeling? With your ax?" the old jailer asked, alluding to Eiden's death.

For a moment, Joss remembered all the times Quinn had doubted her capabilities, especially when it came to beheading horizontally, usually with a sword. He thought he was saving her, and that was partly true. The other part was because he never thought she could do it.

Joss smiled a little, finding she had long since proven him wrong. "I didn't have a sword available," she quipped with a shrug.

Quinn stared at her before a chuckle broke out, finding humor not only in her off-handed comment but in his own misjudging. It was one of the few times he was glad he had been so wrong.

Draping his arm around both her shoulder and Henrik's, he pulled them in closer while asking, "So, what's next for you two?"

"I'm not sure," Henrik admitted, looking to Joss for help.

"I'm sure it'll come to us," she reassured him.

Quinn hugged them again. "Well, there's always someone to

doctor up around here, if you need something to do. As for me, I have a desk to clean out."

With that, he patted them on the back and took off to the jailhouse, whistling a tune they had never heard before, a pep in his step they had never seen.

"What *are* we going to do?" Henrik asked after they collected their horses, mounting into the saddles. Being positive in front of Quinn was one thing, but now his own self-doubt was showing.

Joss could have listed a few things—stop by Hodgson's house to thank him, help organize what the knights were currently unloading from the wagon back at the cottage—but they were all temporary. In the long run, she wasn't quite sure.

"We'll figure it out," she encouraged, pushing Drakon forward through the town's bustling streets, Henrik keeping pace on Bluebelle.

Although Galmoor hadn't changed in the time they were gone, things felt different. Even with her healed wounds—her leg and shoulder healing to a light pink scar—something had shifted, an old life gone and a new one beginning.

The canal town was just as active as when they had left. The waterwheels still turned in the waterways, fueling the electricity powering the streets and buildings. But as they rode among the traffic, people stepped out of their way; vendors called to them, ladies smiled and men said good morning, children were allowed to wave.

It wasn't until someone crossed their path that Henrik's stature suddenly changed, his smile gone.

Joss never thought she'd see Elora Tansy again, but there she was, crossing the street. Looking from her to Henrik, Joss found that despite what happened, his feelings for her hadn't fully been subdued. The betrayal hadn't either, or the memory of what she had been an accomplice to, but his crush wasn't dying easily. He had a stubborn heart that was taking a little longer to heal.

Elora looked up when someone called out to Joss, wishing her well, and seeing the ex-deathsman made her quickly look away as she picked up the pace. Joss stared after her, watching as the girl glanced back only once to make sure she wasn't being followed.

She never looked in Henrik's direction.

"Good riddance."

Joss glanced at Henrik, barely hearing the words uttered under his breath.

They moved on, passing streets and bridges until reaching the edge of town. Crossing the last bridge, the water rushing past in its familiar way, Joss found herself looking over in the direction of the burned down waterwheel mill. She barely saw the gap in the structures of where it lay, the ruins still not fixed. It wasn't until they reached the dirt road to go home that she could see the ledge where she had fallen, both into the rushing river and in love with a man who had yet to return.

The first day home was eventful.

The wagon had been cleared, the knights said their goodbyes and well-wishes, and Joss and Henrik were left to the task of organizing their home to make room for the new food and supplies. Before the knights completely left, however, they had gone with Joss and Henrik to Hodgson's farm, delivering half the goods to the poor farmer and his family as a thank you for all their help, along with the saddlebags and supplies they had borrowed.

While Hodgson insisted they couldn't take the goods from them, he nor his wife could stop the knights from unloading the wagon, forcing them to accept the gifts while both Joss and Henrik observed the scene with smiles.

The second day home was equally busy.

While Hodgson and his sons had done an excellent job of watching the cottage for them, there were still chores to be done. A knock on the door sent Joss's heart into her throat, assuming it was Aric, finally returned. But upon opening the door, she found it to be a farmer's wife from down the road who came to ask for help.

"I burned my hand yesterday, and the salve the doctor gave me isn't working," she was saying, after much apologizing for disturbing them. "I have a friend who said you have a mixture that did wonders for her."

Joss rummaged through her jars, finding the mixture she kept on hand was still decent. "Here, put this on tonight as well and keep it wrapped," she said, after applying a coating to the wound and then handing her the jar. She showed the woman how to wrap it with some bindings she had, and then sent her on her way.

That evening, they were invited to Hodgson's house, where Mrs. Hodgson made a feast with the food they gave them. They spent the night telling them about their travels, saving the more gruesome details for after the children were put to bed.

The third day home would have been quieter if it wasn't for the handful of people who showed up asking for help. A butcher who had cut his arm; a little boy who had fallen from a tree and cut his leg, his mother frantic with worry; a rider who had been dragged by his horse, causing rashes and contusions. While Joss worked to put these people back together, Henrik moved about in the background, checking tonics and concoctions to make sure they were good, and creating more that were becoming sparse. While she stitched wounds, he ground herbs; while he cleaned wounds, she prepared the remedies. The two worked side by side, helping people who had, for most of their lives, ignored them. It also helped that Callan had given them a good supply of undiluted Thymelock. Joss smiled each time she saw the salve, seeing Callan's subtle nudge at them to continue being healers.

The fourth day home was a little more relaxing, although a couple more people stopped by with minor injuries that needed to be attended to.

Despite the company, the two both spent most of the day focusing on cleaning certain aspects of the cottage, taking time for things they usually had to rush through due to preparing for executions. While Henrik was outside cleaning the stable, Joss went to the desk sitting under the window. Rolling up the lid, she pulled open the drawers and gathered the old rejections they had received over the years. She rubbed her thumb over her father's name, remembering what Henrik told her while they were being pardoned. She smiled in memory, of hearing the confession amongst all the "agrees."

But then Aric came to mind, remembering how the desk had been left open, how she confronted him in the bedroom just off to the side. He had stood in that same spot, read these rejections, learning who she really was. Others had too, but he was the only one who stayed.

Looking out the window, her mind recalled how he looked waving to her in that very spot the morning before Callan's execution; how she waved back, hopeful in wanting to spend another evening with him, right before everything changed.

By the fifth day home, both Joss and Henrik were bored.

Joss dressed like she normally did, lacing up her vest, pulling on her boots. Coming down the stairs, she found Henrik making porridge. It wasn't until she went to the closet, grabbing the handle of the ax to prep it that she stopped, realizing the routine she once had was gone. Despite getting everything she wished for, she never expected that she'd feel a little lost afterwards.

No one came to visit that day, and both Joss and Henrik found themselves sitting at the table doing absolutely nothing. Joss sat back in her chair; Henrik had his arms folded on the table, his chin resting on them. They had already done all their chores, had cleaned the cottage to a shine, but now they didn't know what to do. The lifestyle they had built all those years while working for the jailhouse was gone, and it wasn't until they were left sitting in silence that they were faced with a tough reality: while losing the darkest part of their life, they also lost their purpose. No one needed them, no one called for them. They were back to being alone.

What made it worse for Joss was the fact Aric still hadn't returned.

"We could go into town, browse the shops," Henrik offered. "We've never been able to do that before."

What if he stops by when we're not here, she thought. "Yeah, we could," she said instead, knowing she shouldn't wait around for something to happen, like a knock at the door, a reunion she was counting on.

Seeing she really wasn't interested, Henrik tried again. "We could go scout for some land. Start thinking of what to plant for next year."

Joss smiled. "Might be better to do that more towards spring," she replied, eyeing the window, thinking she saw movement but found it was only a bird flying off a branch.

Henrik brought his hand out to rest on the table, drumming the fingers to a beat that was all his own. "I heard there's a cold already starting up. We could harvest some herbs, make some tonics in case more people show up."

Joss brought her gaze to rest on the floor. "That's a good idea. We can get ahead of it."

Neither of them moved; not until a soft knock came from the door, startling them both.

Someone was out there, her mind raced, getting to her feet and approaching the door. Swinging it open, she found a young woman staring back. Her deep green eyes were round, showing her nervousness as her light russet hair fell in waves down her shoulders, almost to her elbows. While her dress was simple, she was cute in a way, though her features seemed a little familiar; Joss couldn't quite place it.

"Hi, Miss Brevyn?" the woman asked.

Joss smiled as she greeted her.

"I'm so sorry to bother you, but my uncle sent me to deliver a message since we're heading into town." She motioned to the road where her ride was waiting for her.

"Your uncle?" Joss asked, feeling Henrik approach out of curiosity.

She saw the girl's eyes go a little wider, staring at the lad in a way that made Joss raise her eyebrow, looking at Henrik to see what the fuss was all about.

"I—I'm Clara's niece. Her sister's daughter," the woman introduced, waking up from whatever spell she had fallen under. When she found the two staring at her confused, she tried again. "Mrs. Hodgson?"

"Oh!" Joss and Henrik exclaimed, both feeling embarrassed that they never remembered Hodgson's wife's name. Out of respect, they only ever called her Mrs. Hodgson. "What does he need?" Joss asked, watching as the girl stared at Henrik again before realizing she was the one being asked.

"He wanted to invite you to a drink at the tavern. The Lazy Ox, he called it. He and a couple of others wanted to hear more about your travels. He asked if you'd be able to stop in around supper."

Joss noted how the girl's eyes kept shifting back to Henrik, realizing she knew that look. At first Joss tried to hide her grin, but then she almost full-on frowned when she saw how oblivious Henrik was to the girl's attractions.

"Of course," Joss agreed when Henrik didn't speak up despite the question being more aimed at him.

"Perfect!" the young woman smiled, before realizing she had nothing more to say. "Well, then, I'll see you two there."

Not knowing what to do with herself, she turned and made her way back down the path.

"Wait, what was your name?" Joss called after her, making her skid to a stop.

"Oh! Sorry, my name is Macie," she smiled. "Macie Tamryn."

"Very nice to meet you," Joss called back. Henrik had already waved and gone back to the table, unfazed by the encounter.

Closing the door, Joss meandered back to her chair. "So, she's cute," she commented. "Seems very sweet."

"Yeah, I guess," Henrik replied, who pulled out his knife to dig some dirt out from underneath his fingernail, resuming his role of being bored. While it didn't bother her to see the knife again, Joss still absentmindedly rubbed the wound on her shoulder, reminding herself that her injury was nothing more than a scar now. The threat was long over.

Watching Henrik for a bit, Joss found no other reaction to be had. "Well, since it sounds like a special occasion," she stated, "Why don't you go put on one of those nice shirts Callan gave you?"

"Why? It's just a tavern," Henrik shrugged, clearly not getting it.

Her tone came out a little more forceful. "Go put on one of those nice shirts Callan gave you."

"Fine, then," Henrik scoffed, putting his knife away as he got up from the table and made his way upstairs.

Smiling after him, Joss remained at the table, drumming her fingers on the wood and reliving the look she saw on Macie's face. Henrik deserved that kind of look, if only he had noticed it.

As she sat there, she recalled where she had seen that look

before: on someone who played chess with her at that very table, who promised to come find her, but had yet to arrive.

CHAPTER TWENTY-EIGHT

The Lazy Ox looked no different except for the quantity of horses tied out front, much more than they usually saw. Joss and Henrik didn't think too much of it until they entered and found to their surprise a full tavern filled with applause, all attention on them.

Both stood in the doorway, too used to slipping in undetected that being the center of attention had stunned them. It took Hodgson to come forward, stepping behind and pushing them gently along for both Joss and Henrik to move to the table in the center of the room.

"What's all this for?" Joss asked, people patting her shoulder and arm as she passed, wishing her well as she moved. She found they were doing the same to Henrik.

"You two," Hodgson admitted.

"What, for saving the king?" Henrik laughed, knowing half these people didn't like politics and the other half wouldn't have been able to point out Callan in a crowd if they were paid to.

"You'll see," Hodgson winked, stepping back over to the bar.

At first, they assumed everyone was there to bask in the glory of the two ex-outcasts. They were the only two people who had ever been deemed heroes in a town with more crime than nobility. But as people started coming up to them, the two realized very quickly that this wasn't a welcome home party or a reunion of any sort.

Each person there came to say the "thank you" they had never come back to say, their courage marred by the fact that they had gone to a deathsman for help. Now, with the title lifted, they had come to right their wrongs, spilling out the gratitude that for some had taken years to say. Some said it with tears, others with drawn out explanations. Despite the fact neither Joss nor Henrik had ever expected to be thanked—even long writing it off—it began to settle in the more people talked, the more they squeezed their shoulders and shook their hands. Some, especially the older ones, spoke of her father, how they admired his professionalism, how often they admired her for following diligently in his skill. These words made her think of Callan's reasoning for not wanting to pardon her, seeing for the first time how much of what she did had mattered.

In between these friendly exchanges, the first round of ale came from Garrett himself, the tavern keeper who had never given them the warmest welcomes whenever they came around. But for the first time, he squeezed her shoulder, smiling at her in a job well done she never received before. The second round came from Macie, who Joss knew had taken it upon herself to bring it by, given how often she looked at Henrik throughout the evening. It helped that the shirt he wore from Callan was a deep forest green, a shade that lightened his eyes and stood out against his tousled brown hair. There were a couple of other women who had turned a second time to eye him.

Searching Hodgson out, Joss gave him a knowing smile when he caught her gaze, onto his attempts at trying to be a matchmaker. He simply smiled back, raising his frothy mug in a sort of "I did good" salute, causing her to stifle a laugh.

"So, Macie," Joss asked, pulling the girl's attention when Henrik started conversing with another local. "What brings you to Galmoor?"

"Well," Macie said, a pretty smile lighting up her face, "Aunt Clara is a wonderful seamstress, so I was hoping to stay a few weeks so she could teach me how to sew a little bit better. My mother is so busy with our store in Brenton that she said it would be best to learn from my aunt."

Joss nodded, remembering all the shirts Mrs. Hodgson helped sew for them, little favors that hadn't seemed so big until they were pointed out. "She is wonderful," she complimented. "You'll definitely learn from the best. Is there anything you're planning on doing with that knowledge?"

"I'm planning to be a dressmaker," she admitted proudly. That's when she pulled out a dainty lace handkerchief, so delicately made that Joss was almost afraid to touch it.

"You made this?" Joss asked, surprised by its elegance. It was something she could see adorning a lady in Aselian among all the beauty and finery.

"Yes." Macie's face brightened further, which was becoming contagious. "I need to get a little bit better about the edges, but I was hoping to add this kind of design to the dresses. A practical dress can also be elegant," she reasoned.

Joss agreed, though side-eyed Henrik who was enjoying his ale and not really paying attention now that the local had moved on to other conversations.

"It's beautiful," Joss complimented. "Don't you think, Henrik?"

The lad, in mid swig, nodded in agreement, though he only glanced at it.

A little disheartened by his disinterest, Macie quietly put the handkerchief away. "I should probably go see if my uncle needs anything," she said, still smiling, though Joss caught the rejection there.

While she took a swig of her ale, Joss's eyes narrowed on Henrik, and when her foot found its mark and he jumped, she put the mug down like nothing had happened.

"What was that for?" Henrik whispered harshly, rubbing his leg.

"You need to be nice to her," Joss whispered back. "She's ambitious, sweet, and smitten with you. At least be nice back."

Henrik looked down at the table, still rubbing his leg.

"I know it's because of Elora."

Henrik's eyes met her gaze, the guilt flooding into his stare. Given that he was such an inquisitive and thoughtful person, the fact he wouldn't acknowledge the handkerchief or Macie's hard work had given him away. He wasn't being oblivious; he was avoiding.

"Listen," Joss said gently, "you're allowed to be mad; you're allowed to be hurt. You have every right to be. But you're not allowed to be cruel."

It was a harsh word to use, but she needed to get the point across, not wanting his heartbreak to ruin him. Joss watched as Henrik sat back in his chair, tapping his finger on the mug. She could see his mind working, but instead of saying anything more, she sat with him in his silence. A song picked up around them, people becoming lost in the melody.

"It was a pretty handkerchief," she heard Henrik admit before his gaze went to Macie and then back to the table.

"Hey," Joss spoke up, gaining his attention. "Just go talk to her, introduce yourself properly. It doesn't have to become any-thing right now except a friendly conversation."

Henrik thought it over, and with a nod and his lop-sided smile, he got up from the table and made his way to the bar.

Joss sat back, enjoying the ale as she watched the patrons sing-ing around her, joining in a couple of times to the parts of the song she knew. In between the lyrics, she sneaked looks at Henrik, watching as a very shy introduction unfold into a conversation that had him smiling, even running a hand through his hair as Macie stared up at him with sparkling eyes. As the song shifted to a different one, Joss continued to drink her ale and enjoy the atmosphere.

And then, as another round of ales was being passed, Joss, by accident, caught sight of the Lost Wall. She wasn't sure why she looked over—perhaps just out of habit—but her stomach knotted in its familiar way, the flyers and parchments sobering her from the fuzzy gaiety surrounding her. Looking at it was like looking at an old memory, a tingle of the pain resurfacing like a muscle ache.

There was one person she didn't have to look for anymore,

and one she was afraid to find.

The days droned slowly on, autumn settling in around them with the turning colors of the leaves and the bouts of rain. A fortnight passed, and still Aric hadn't come back. There were plenty of knocks, many people wanting to help, but no signs of the man with the different colored eyes.

The hardest part was the waiting; looking out the window throughout the day, wondering if she would see him out there looking in, or making his way down the lane, or knocking on the door in the dead of night. Each day passed and nothing happened, and still she waited.

However, in those passing days, two frequent visitors did show up: Macie, who, with Henrik's help, had come up with almost every excuse to spend the day with them, which always ended up with her and Henrik in some deep conversation that Joss usually had to see herself out of; and Quinn, who had come up with an idea of his own.

"Expand the cottage," he said, coming to the table one morning and rolling out the blank parchment.

Joss, who was preparing to go to the stream to do their laundry, sat the basket on a chair. "And why do that?" she asked.

"Look at you: all the money in the world now and you still take your dirty laundry out to the creek when you could build a proper washroom. You can do better." Quinn pointed his finger up, literally making a point of the fact.

"Winter is coming. Isn't that the worst time to be building?"

"Not necessarily," Quinn commented, though it was Henrik

who noted the worry in Joss's face.

The cottage was the last of their old life that was untouched. While there had been a lot of heartache, there had been happiness as well. Joss had helped raise her siblings, and Henrik, within those walls. She had kept the roof over their heads when her father couldn't. Seeing those walls removed was going to be uncomfortable.

"It'll take a while to devise a plan," Henrik gently reminded her. "We can just play with the idea, and if we don't like it, then we won't do it."

Joss nodded in understanding. Grabbing the basket, she proceeded out the door.

"How did you get into building, anyway?" she heard Henrik ask Quinn.

"A man can have hobbies," the older man rebuked as she shut the door quietly behind her.

Following the path, she trudged through the open field, birds chirping around as her boots crunched through the wet grass. If she allowed herself, she could picture that day, the wildflowers scattered around, a cricket chirping nearby as she and Aric had made their way to the creek.

Remodeling the cottage really wasn't the problem; it was losing moments like this, retracing steps that had become fond memories. She would be losing the room he had been lying in or the wash closet, where she had seen the full extent of his body before helping him into the bath. Changing the scenery meant he was officially gone.

Reaching the end of the field, she came to the blackberry bushes standing guard underneath the tangling trees. Following the small trail that wound around it, she heard the trickling of water as she carefully side-stepped the thorny vines. Finally, she came to the wide and lazy creek, the smooth rocks still lining the way in random spots. Her eyes automatically went to the way it made a jagged bridge, remembering how Aric had crossed it; how he slipped, how he ended up okay.

Shaking her head, she moved down the dirt embankment and onto one of the rocks. Despite the rains, the creek was still mild in temper, not yet swelling and overtaking her spot. Setting the basket down, she picked up the soap, the scent of lemon and lavender lingering in the air as she grabbed one of her shirts.

As she scrubbed and washed, her eyes occasionally glanced up, checking the embankment across the way. It was a normal routine, being aware of her surroundings just in case, but at that moment, she was reliving things. The way he had stood in the light on the other side of the embankment; the way he stood when he had aimed his crossbow at her; the way he held onto her on that ledge; the way he promised to find her before he turned away in the crowd.

He must be dead, she reasoned. True, there was the dark shadow on the balcony with the perfect aim who struck Eiden down without a second thought. There was also the mysterious archer who had helped the knights win against the barricade at the doors. But there was also the hair, and his absence. Maybe the dark figure was just another rogue, seeking their own vengeance. That was almost a better thought, a better excuse to why Aric hadn't returned. Eiden had told the truth about a lot of things. Maybe Aric's death had been one of them.

Joss scrubbed the shirt, her vision blurring. *No, death is better,* she told herself, wringing the shirt out, trying to hold herself together as she folded the shirt and sat it down next to her before reaching for another one.

Death meant he would have come back if he had been able to.

Death meant he would have kept his promise.

If he wasn't dead, it meant his absence was a choice, and it was that thought which caused the tears to spill over as she scrubbed. It meant someone else would have removed his stitches in his thigh and shoulder; someone else was enjoying his company over chess or ale or even in bed. It meant that even after being pardoned—after saving a king—she still wasn't good enough. If, by chance, he was that dark shadow on the balcony who had saved her, that had been his payment for her saving him. That had been his goodbye.

Everyone leaves.

Dunking the shirt in the water, she wiped the tears with the back of her hand, letting the emotions come as she worked. It was better she cried here instead of at home anyway, where no one could see.

It took a while, but eventually the clothes were cleaned and folded, put back in the basket for transporting. As Joss stood up, knees sore from kneeling and the basket heavier in hand, she felt the first few drops of rain. Looking up, she found the grey storm clouds had returned, not realizing the sun had long been blocked out.

Wiping the last of the tears and taking a reassuring breath, Joss made her way back up the embankment and through the blackberry bushes. The wind picked up then, and as the cold chill hit her back, she wished she had remembered to bring her cloak.

Re-entering the open field, she trudged forward, the heaviness of the basket slowing her down.

See? We make a good team.

She swallowed the lump in her throat as she shifted the basket to get a better grip. Aric's words still hummed in her mind, though, the memory of him helping her carry the basket returning as she walked the same path alone.

As she trudged on, trying to hurry against the rain that was now steadily coming down, she noticed something breaking through the far line of trees and undergrowth: a horse and cloaked rider appearing at a trot. At first, Henrik came to mind, coming to get her from the storm. But then she realized the horse was a chestnut, not a dark brown like Drakon or blue roan like Bluebelle.

Watching the rider catch sight of her, moving the horse down to a brisk walk, she found herself coming to a stop as the world seemed to pause around her. She recognized that horse, and then she saw the crossbow snug against the rider's back.

Pulling the horse down to a stop a few paces from her, Aric lifted his hood off despite the rain, his long wavy blonde hair spilling over his shoulders in the familiar way it did. A cut swollen under his eye showed he had had a hell of a time getting back, but the way he looked at her was clear: the urgency, the wanting.

Dismounting, Aric walked a few steps before coming to a stop, staring back at the woman who hadn't moved, her face consumed in shock.

"I'm not *too* late, am I?" he asked.

The basket slipped from Joss's hands, landing with a thud in the grass as she ran to him, her arms already around his neck as he caught her. Falling to his knees, he took her with him, holding onto her as the rain came down around.

"You came back," Joss whispered, her body trembling against the warmth of his embrace.

He buried his face in her hair, breathing her scent in. "Of course I came back," he whispered in return. "You can't get rid of me that easily."

He wanted to tell her everything: the fiasco at the doors of the Great Hall; the way he hunted them up into the training grounds; how those masked fools hid in the very place they had trained, only to be picked off one by one. It had been hell in its own right, but he saw it through. However, when he pulled back, seeing her face and those tears he caused, he was too busy with her lips to speak, kissing her in the same way he had on the ledge.

The greediness of that kiss spoke for both, keeping them warm as the rain soaked them through. And when their lips finally parted, the lightning and thunder overhead interrupting them, neither could let go; not yet, not when they had both spent so long in wanting this moment.

After another crack of lightning, and the rain drenching every part of them, the two came to their feet, Joss gathering the basket while Aric collected his horse. As they made their way back to the cottage, Aric took the other handle so that the basket hung in between them. They fell into step together, keeping the same pace as the silence became comfortable between them.

Aric would eventually tell her everything, as Joss would, over dinner and then while in bed tangled under sheets. They would fill in the gaps with the missing pieces: how he had killed off the Mask's men like he vowed; how she and Henrik were pardoned, and spoiled, by Callan; how he had worried about her; how she had missed him.

For now, though, they walked quietly through the field together, both wanting to be there, needing the same type of company.

Because this was their love story.

Neither of them would have wanted it any other way.

EPILOGUE

The best time to attend the cathedral was always at night, especially for a queen.

With two guards at her flank, Muriel made her way down the nave, keeping her footsteps as quiet as possible so as not to disturb the handful of people who were already inside praying. It was hard staying silent, her deep navy dress sliding behind her and the guards' armor clinking a little, though they did their best to walk lightly. Heads still lifted, bows were exchanged, and Muriel continued uninterrupted.

Reaching the crossing, she turned to face the rows of small candles, approaching as she looked upon the stained-glass window of the rose. The rain clouds had parted over the evening, causing the moonlight to project through the glass, giving it a faint glow.

She still came to the cathedral each day to light the candles, but instead of lighting one in desperation, she lit four in gratitude—Callan, for making it home; Joss and Henrik, for being the heroes that they were; and to Aric Kayden, the man she had never met but heard all about, whose change of heart she couldn't ignore.

As she stared at the little flames dancing before her, she noticed something wedged in between two candles near the top. Reaching for it, she found it was a small strip of paper, just missing the melted wax around it.

Muriel smiled even before she read the words etched in ink: *Leirum U Oye Voli.*

She had no idea when Callan had the time to place it there, but she couldn't contain the way her smile widened. Even when the footsteps came up behind her, she was still glowing from the inside out when she turned to meet the page.

"His Majesty is requesting your presence on the battlements, Your Majesty," he bowed.

The meeting had run late, but the note he left made up for it. She nodded to him, following him out as the guards remained behind her.

Leaving the cathedral, Muriel made her way down the steps to the waiting carriage. Taking her place inside, the page closed the door and signaled to the driver as her two guards pulled themselves up on the back of the carriage, always watchful. Her body swayed with the movement of the horses as they trotted along down the road. A stream of moonlight entered through the window, and Muriel used it to look at the note again, reading the words over and over.

Upon passing through the gates, the carriage swung around, coming to a rolling stop. The door opened, and she was guided out by the page who had given her his hand. Following the page, she noticed her two guards remaining behind.

"He asked to see you alone, Your Majesty," the page answered her, seeing how she was looking back.

Following up the wide staircase, she found Callan on the top of the battlement, guards standing at attention across the wall, stationed in between the lit torches. He still dressed in black, keeping to the mourning ritual a little longer than the rest, and despite not wearing the crown, he stood very much like a king. Sleep had awakened the youth in him, his dark eyes spirited as he traced his gaze over her form, taking in the navy dress, the intricate detailing of her bodice, the jewels glistening in the torchlight.

"Late night for you," Callan grinned as she approached.

"I wasn't able to go earlier," she explained, bowing before taking his hand. "Queens get busy too."

Callan's smile deepened as he gently moved her hand to his arm, escorting her across the wall. "Well, I hate to take you from your busy schedule, Your Majesty. I figured with the rains clearing, we could enjoy the night for a moment."

Muriel smiled at him. "That's a wonderful idea, given how busy you've been as well." She held up the paper then, causing him to laugh a little.

As they walked, neither said anything more. Muriel kept her eyes on the sky, admiring the stars. The air still held the freshness of rain, and she breathed in despite the chill that caused goosebumps to rise against her arms even through her cloak. Glancing at Callan, she found a smile remaining on his lips while he kept a lookout, as if anticipating something.

He had told her about those last five years, and in the horror of hearing it, she found understanding: why he was always watching his surroundings; why he had a hard time sleeping some nights, sounds always waking him that she never heard; why he had a hard time trusting people, assuming the worst. And she had seen his scars, kissing each one when given the chance. Muriel knew she couldn't always help him, but she did know she could at least love him through it.

They continued their stroll in silence, walking the length of the battlements until they reached the area where the lake was, the water lapping against the stone wall. Here, the guards were stretched further out, giving them a place to be alone. In the distance, the workings of the waterwheels echoed into the stillness, illuminating the castle and city behind them. While clouds were still spaced out overhead, a full moon cast its white light against the dark waters. A breeze picked up again, and Muriel pulled her cloak closer as she huddled to Callan for warmth.

"Your meeting ran longer than normal," she mentioned as they came to a stop, admiring the view.

"It was about the training grounds again," he admitted, his voice a little quieter than before. "They keep finding bodies."

Muriel looked at him, seeing the sternness outlined in his face. He hadn't kept any of the meetings from her, divulging the days' duties to her like a diary. The attack on the training grounds, however, had been a surprise to her while something in him had expected it. "Do you think it was *him?*" she asked, thinking of that fourth candle she lit, for the man she hadn't met but had changed her life just the same.

"I have my suspicions." Callan kept his eyes on the water. The fact the reports claimed the bodies had masks on or within their possession told him exactly who had done it. The arrows alone had given Aric Kayden away.

"You declared him dead, though," she reminded him. When

the body was found in the tunnels, the one belonging to the hair that Eiden had revealed, Callan didn't hesitate in confirming it was Aric. In fact, he had been generous about the fact, not even breaking character for Muriel.

Now it was a different story, seeing the way he was smiling at her. "I did," he said. "And even if I was, say, exaggerating the truth, you know how people gossip around here."

She knew all too well how people eavesdropped. And with a lost prince returned, the eagerness to know more about him and the attacks on the royal family only increased their appetites. It didn't help when the bodies were found in Traitor's Alley, or at the training ground.

"You're protecting him," she whispered, finding she was right by how he winked at her. Still, he wouldn't admit it, not even alone on the wall with only her around.

Muriel pressed her lips together in response to his silence. Then, with a shake of her head, she said, "Why do you always have to be so theatrical?"

A laugh escaped him. "Because you know you adore it," Callan teased.

"Oh, please." Muriel shook her head, feigning victimhood. "Like with Joss and Henrik, you could have easily pardoned them. They deserved that pardon from you. But no, you had to go through a whole production involving the council."

"Yes, I did," he agreed, his smile never wavering from remembering his own cleverness. "For them, I did."

"What do you mean?" Muriel asked, tired of his vagueness.

"It wasn't just about being pardoned. It was about acceptance.

They were shunned their whole life, Muriel. I wanted them to know that they meant something, not just to me but to the whole of our realm. I didn't plan on the crowd joining in, though. That... was truly for them."

Muriel still recalled that day, her heart still light with joy, seeing the way the two held onto each other, their fate finally changed. "What if the council had said no?" she asked, reminding him that he had played a dangerous game.

"Then we'd have a new council."

"You're reckless," she accused, though the curve of her lips showed it was more of a tease.

"Even if they said no, it wouldn't have meant much. I had already notified the towns of their pardon a week before," Callan admitted, breaking into a laugh when Muriel's gasp filled the air between them.

"Scoundrel!"

"Loveable scoundrel," he corrected her.

"Alright then, say it to my face," she declared, coming to stand right in front of him, making him look into her eyes.

Being this close was dangerous and Callan knew once he started kissing her it would be the end of them on that wall, scandals rising from how indecent they would become.

"Tell me Aric Kayden is dead," she said. "Truly mean it."

"Aric Kayden is dead, for his own sake," he said, something soft crossing his face, "and for hers."

Muriel's pointed look slowly softened upon hearing the confession, realizing he wasn't lying just to protect Aric, assuming it was a debt being paid after not assassinating him. Instead, he was lying for Joss, to give her a man who wouldn't be hunted for past crimes.

"She loves him," Muriel whispered, finding she liked this truth a little more, that she would have kept the secret as well, even from Callan, if the roles had been reversed.

"He loves her more," Callan reasoned, who had already picked up on the signs. At first, it had been an annoyance, given that Aric was supposed to kill him. But their sad reality had gotten to him, so lying about the body being Aric's when it clearly wasn't had been his way of thanking them both, to give them the happily ever after they deserved.

"You *are* a loveable scoundrel," she whispered, seeing the romantic in him, the side of him that left notes among candles and blood-stained words on cloth.

Touching her nose with his, Callan couldn't take it anymore. "Let's go inside," he whispered, and in his deep tone she knew exactly why, wanting the same thing.

Smiling, Muriel moved around him, taking a couple steps forward, assuming he'd follow. But when she looked over her shoulder, she found Callan staring across the lake at the hills in the distance. Following his gaze, she knew what direction he was looking in: where a poor canal town sat, a new life beginning for three deserving souls.

Underneath the moonlight, Muriel watched as Callan kissed two fingers and then placed them over his heart, bowing his head in their direction. She understood what the gesture meant, and she loved him more for it. And when he came to her side, squeezing her hand as they made their way back through the battlements, that gesture remained in her mind, settling into a memory.

It was a sign of respect, an acknowledgment to the friends he'd always consider family.

It was an affectionate goodbye until they'd one day meet again.

ACKNOWLEDGMENTS

Personally, I'm not the biggest fan of endings. Whether in real life or in writing, once I develop that repour with someone (or character), I never really want things to end. I never imagine an ending until I'm already faced with it. So when it came time to write this final book, I tried to be as mentally prepared as possible. I went in with a full outline, accepting that this was the last book and that I needed to do these characters justice. But what I didn't expect was that despite all of my planning, I still ended up crying like a baby in those last chapters, particularly the final fight, the pardoning, Joss and Aric's reunion, and those last words in the epilogue. Those were the moments that I realized how important these characters were to me and how I wouldn't be writing with them anymore after this. While I will never rule out a continuation of their story, for now they'll get to have their happily ever afters that they deserve. Just like the last sentence, this is my affectionate goodbye to these characters until we'll one day meet again.

Overall, I have to say to all my friends, family, coworkers, and online book community a very grateful thank you for supporting my work. I'm beyond blessed to have such an amazing tribe who continuously cheers me on and encourages my storytelling. I sincerely thank you all and hope I continue to make you proud.

For this story in particular, a special thank you goes to Eleanor at North Pines Editing, LLC, for her amazing help, input, and wonderful support in both editing and sharing this story; to Gina, my forever editor and writing partner-in-crime, for always being there to help me restructure and tidy things up, for finding details I missed, and for the best reactions when it came to some of these scenes; to my mom, Rhonda, for always being there and cheering me on when I need it; to Jess, this trilogy's first fan, who has been an amazing beta reader and friend; and to my husband, Alex, for your unwavering support and encouragement, and for always believing in me, especially on those days that I couldn't.

And to you, lovely reader: thank you for reading these books and for reaching the end of this road with me. I hope you enjoyed the journey with Joss and Aric as much as I did.

Now, on to the next adventure!

ABOUT THE AUTHOR

A. M. Dunnewin grew up with a taste for mysteries and thrillers, inherited ever so lovingly from her family. An affiliate member of the Horror Writers Association, A. M.'s own stories cover a wide range of genres that tend to take a dark turn when least expected. With a B.A. in Psychology, she's a gambler of words, obsessed with chai tea, and addicted to books—everything from classical literature to graphic novels. Other hobbies include art, history, music, equestrianism, and a good classic film. She currently dwells in Northern California.

www.ingramcontent.com/pod-product-compliance
Lightning Source LLC
Chambersburg PA
CBHW060708190726
48289CB00002B/593

9 781952 577192